CUTTER

j. woodburn barney

An AppalachianAcorn Book

ISBN: 0692441077
ISBN-13: 978-0692441077

Published by AppalachianAcorn

Cover design and illustration by Vicki Moon Spiegel

for Deborah

"Many men go fishing all of their lives
without knowing that it is not fish they are after."

Henry David Thoreau

CUTTER

ONE

He was having the dream again. The hard plastic chair. The faded blue wall. The huge clock with the irritating click, click, click of the second hand. The fear and anger, though he couldn't quite identify the source. Nobody to ask.

Now a new sound coming from the clock. A buzzing. But that doesn't fit the dream.

Shit. Alarm. Cell phone.

He fumbled the phone off the nightstand and onto the floor. Retrieved it. Tapped the screen until he managed to hit the snooze.

Aaaahhh.

Something's not right. Wait. On vacation. At the Outer Banks. Why was the fucking alarm going off? Mistake.

Aaaahhh.

Shit. Gotta be at Oden's Dock at 7:00 a.m. Fucking Clint and his rah-rah, team-building, fucking fishing trip. What a crock.

Cutter found the lamp switch, turned it on and his eyes adjusted to the bright whites and yellows of the condo room.

And he rolled out of bed. Literally.

The room was standard Hatteras Island fare. Not old Hatteras. That would have been concrete block walls, painted sea mist green. Window air conditioner. Black mold in the bathroom. Two year old fish scales on the floor under the bed. Odors that told stories of the guys who drank and smoked and played poker and lied to each other about the fish they didn't catch that day. No, this was the modern Outer Banks. Bright colors and cheap prints of the Hatteras Lighthouse and seagulls. A big plastic fish on the wall over the couch. And lamps filled with seashells.

Two bedrooms. Though Cutter was alone. Wasn't anything smaller available. As he did every morning, he touched his toes, just to make sure everything was still working, scratched his balls through his boxers and shuffled, first to the bathroom, and then to the kitchen to make coffee.

Let's see. Thirty minutes to get there. Stop at the Orange Blossom for one of those apple ugly thingies, ten minutes. Forty-five minutes. Almost time to rock and roll.

Cutter was early thirties, mostly nondescript. In so many ways. Average height, average weight, average looks. The only noticeable features were the dorky, black-rimmed glasses he always wore and the unruly shock of blond hair. It was thick and curly, not in the wavy way, but in the frizzy Brillo-pad way. Through his teen years he fought it on a daily basis, trying to tame it into one of the fashionable looks, but by college he had surrendered, thrown in the towel, said "Fuck it" and let it be whatever it wanted to be.

Today it wanted to be multi-tufted, its traditional salt-air, slept-in look. But nothing his favorite Red Sox ball cap wouldn't cover.

So while the coffee maker hissed its way through its assigned duty, Cutter brushed his teeth, found a pair of not-too-dirty khaki shorts, a clean tee shirt (the black River Roots one) and his blue chambray shirt and got dressed. And Mr. Coffee finished at exactly the right minute.

Five minutes to drink a cup and...

Ah, shit. Dammit. This Clintfest is overnight. Pack. Get the backpack—trunks, jeans, sweatshirt. Dammit. Toothbrush.

Cutter stuffed his gear into the backpack, closed the sliding glass door to the balcony. Balcony, it was to laugh—ten square feet enclosed by a rusty railing. At the door he went through his departure ritual, touching each item as he repeated the litany, "Watch. Wallet. Keys. Spectacles. Testicles. Cell phone."

Good to go.

Out the door. Into the Wrangler.

He'd had the Jeep about four years. Always wanted one. Got it as a present to himself after the, what would you call it, the lost time. He still wouldn't admit that his brother was right about the car. Jim had told him he wouldn't like it. Bad gas mileage. Terrible seats. Kill your back.

After eighteen hours on the road to get here, his back had been on fire. And his wallet half empty. Still, this place was what the car was built for—four-wheeling on the beach with the top off. Nobody wanted to ride with him back home, but here, on the beach, here all of them wanted a turn behind the wheel.

Out Antilles Road and onto Highway 12, coffee in hand. He wasn't excited about being out with those people during his vacation. But the sun was up, he had Buffett and Dylan to keep him company and he was going deep sea fishing. So it wasn't all that bad.

Past Canadian Hole, into Buxton. Stop for the fritter on steroids—damn tough to eat when a guy has to drink hot coffee and use a stick shift all at once.

Still on time. More traffic than he expected. Must be the Hatteras version of rush hour. All rusted out cars and beat up pickups. Brigand Bay on the right and something on the road. What?

Shit. It's a rooster, strolling slowly across Highway 12.

Why did the chicken cross the road? To show his friends he had guts.

Slow down and let the chicken finish his walk. Apparently he was on his way to work at the Frisco Mini Golf across the road. Just like the ten foot tall fiberglass rooster at the putt-putt at Fort Myers Beach.

He wondered where that photograph was. She had insisted that he pose with that huge plastic chicken. One of his running stories with her was how, when he was growing up with his seven brothers and sisters, the family raised most of its own food, including chickens. And that because they were so poor, the only pet he ever had was a chicken. Named Fred. Who, in late summer, became a family dinner. And how he never wanted another pet. Ever.

She laughed every time he told it. He liked that about her. She had had the photograph enlarged and framed as a gift for him.

He met her—Amanda—when he was hired to do some writing for the private school where she taught science to elementary age students.

Cutter had been brought in to do a professional standards guide for St. Mary of the Light Catholic School for Girls, or as he preferred, St. Mary of the Tight Ass. He had been hired, on recommendation of the Bishop, based on his time working in the purgatory of Human Resources for the Diocese where his parents were regular contributors. Mom and Dad thought that maybe it would be a good thing for him to "give back" to the Church, what with it having provided him with the good education that earned him a scholarship to Northwestern. He thought it would be a good idea to get his parents off his back. Well, that, and it was nigh impossible to get a job with a degree in English.

So he was hired. The job, as it turned out, was to take all the "do's and don't's" the school administration (and, he assumed, all the Catholic hierarchy right up to the Pope) insisted on for the staff and translate it into words and phrases that, if read by the outside world—the internet—wouldn't appear to be the anachronistic view of the world that it really was. Oh, and incidentally, to get staff buy-in to the document. Easy.

His boss, the principal of St. Mary of the Tight Ass, was one Dr. Edward T. Fenton, PhEd. Referred to by the staff as "That fucking Fenton," which Cutter was shocked to discover was not an homage to John Sanford. Dr. Fenton, as he insisted on being called, even by his closest colleagues, was a study in stereotypes—had the stereotype been for a principal from the 1950s—from the flat top haircut with the white sidewalls to his gray suit and white starched shirt to his black wingtip shoes, spit-shined.

Cutter's first day on the job began with a meeting to introduce him to the staff.

"Ladies and gentlemen," started Dr. Fenton, "may I remind you that when we say we begin work at 7:00 a.m. it does NOT mean we arrive at 7:00, take off our coats, get our coffee, chat with our coworkers about last night's TV shows and then begin working. It means we are at our desks commencing work no later than 7:00," eliciting substantial eye rolling from the staff and a barely concealed gag reflex from Cutter.

Fenton continued, "Today we begin work on the updates to our Professional Standards Handbook. This does NOT mean we will be lowering our standards. Is that understood? And His Eminence has decided we could use the assistance of…"

He interrupted himself. "Well, Miss Reagan, I'm so glad you could join us this morning. Although I must point out that you are ten minutes tardy."

"I am so sorry, Dr. Fenton. I stopped at the chapel because I felt I needed to pray a rosary." Amanda blushed slightly. More staff eye rolling. This time Cutter did not gag. In fact, he had the opposite reaction.

And he was more than a little surprised that Fenton did not seem to realize she was pulling his leg.

"Very well, Miss Reagan. Take your seat, but in the future please be mindful to be more punctual." Can this guy be serious?

"As I was saying, I would like to introduce," though he was clearly put out by having this interloper in his domain, "Mr. Winston Williams who will be assisting us in this endeavor. I expect you to cooperate in such a manner that permits Mr. Williams to quickly finish his work. Mr. Williams?"

With that, Cutter stood, adopted his "aw, shucks" persona and addressed the group.

"Hi. Please call me Cutter and…"

Fenton interrupted again, "Mr. Williams, we prefer, here at St. Mary of the Light, to keep things on a professional basis, including using proper titles and last names."

"Oh. Okay. Sorry."

From there the meeting went downhill. Except for being able to look at her.

Over the next few weeks, Cutter spent a lot of time with members of the staff. More than he ordinarily would have. He made his best effort to engage them personally. He knew that he had to get their approval of a document that would be, at best, repugnant to any thinking person born after 1890.

"Good day, old chaps," Cutter rolled out his very proper British accent. At least a couple of them smiled. This group of five elementary teachers, including

Amanda, was meeting in the science room, filled with posters and diagrams—including one that demonstrated how clearly the Big Guy had guided evolution so as not to contradict any Biblical explanations of creation. Quite thoughtful of Him. Cutter looked over the posters of "Our Friends, the Wildlife" and settled on the picture of the beaver and added, again in the strained British, "I say, what attractive and informative posters. I, myself, have always considered the beaver to be one of my favorite friends. Always puts me in mind of fancying a wee bit of the old shag." The female teachers tittered, the male one guffawed.

"Watt? Watt?" Cutter said with his eyebrows raised and chin down, as if he had been completely misconstrued.

This time they laughed. And Amanda, using her best Piccadilly flower girl accent added, "My wood, you sure do got a pair, donya, gubnor?" More laughter.

They got down to work, productive work. This became his favorite group, though he did notice, to his growing dismay, his arrival would frequently result in Amanda's departure. She later told him whenever she heard him arrive, she fled to the women's room to avoid what might come out of his mouth. He took it as a compliment.

One day when the group was at lunch, Amanda asked him, "So, Mr. Winston Williams, why Cutter? Why not Win or, better yet, Winnie?"

"Long story."

"We have time."

Cutter thought a moment, shrugged and told them, "By the time I got to high school—a very Catholic high school, known for turning out only the finest young gentlemen—I had developed a relatively intense aversion to all things educational. Whenever I got the chance, I skipped—morning, noon, even mid-class, I would go to the bathroom and just not go back. Notes to my parents didn't work, detentions didn't deter, a suspension was a reward. Finally the principal had enough and I was given a choice. I could be expelled or I could wear a sign around my neck for thirty days. If I was ever seen without the sign, I would be immediately expelled. I chose, or more correctly, my parents chose the sign. It said 'CUTTER'. Name sort of stuck."

"Oh. Not very inspiring," offered Amanda.

"They can't all be good stories," he replied. "Shall I make one up?"

By early January Cutter finished up his writing and turned it over to the staff for review, recommendations and, hopefully, endorsement. With two dissenting votes (that old prig Mr. Churko who believed Jesus was thinking of him personally when he chose to die on the cross, and dour-faced Mrs. Hunt, the resident guardian of young girls' virtue (who read romance novels at night and touched herself "down there")—his work was heartily endorsed by the staff.

Predictably that fucking Fenton did not like it. At all. He believed it too greatly limited his powers to appropriately deal with the miscreants among the staff. However, at the direction of the Bishop—Yes, Your

Excellency. As you wish—Fenton passed it on to the lait council where it was endorsed and sent to the Bishop for his approval. Which came. Promptly.

Dr. Fenton decided, since Cutter was out of his reach, to punish staff members who had worked with him. Somehow. Some day.

Cutter, for his part, was glad the job was over. Though it meant he wouldn't be working with Amanda, he could at last finally ask her out.

She said no.

The driver of the beat up pickup with the empty boat trailer laid on his horn and jolted Cutter back to attention. The rooster had finally finished his jaunt to work at the putt-putt. Cutter smiled and moved the Jeep along.

TWO

Cutter wheeled into the parking lot at Oden's, backed into a space and was hit by the smell of dead fish. The sea mist and humidity were already being brought to a boil by the sun. It was going to be very warm, at least on land.

"Hey, Cutter-boy!" It was Ken, Clint's lawyer, confidante and sometimes advisor. Cutter liked Ken, at least in small doses, though a female campaign donor, of considerable means, had described Ken as "that little tiny grain of sand which gets into the corner of your eye and irritates the shit out of you." Fair enough.

"Yo!" Cutter answered. Ken was munching a biscuit and egg sandwich from the Harbor Deli and already wearing some of it on his shirt. The shirt, of course, was a $180 Orvis fly fishing special. With all the bells and whistles. SPF 50. Epaulets. Fourteen double stitched pockets. Guaranteed to catch fish. Unless you dropped mustard on it.

As Cutter pulled out his backpack and closed up the Jeep, Ken yelled, "Hey, you know where the ship is parked?" Ken was very nautical. "I can't remember its name."

"HER name is the *Debbie Lee*. And she is a boat. The second biggest at this dock. I'd bet we'll be able to find her."

In fact, the *Debbie Lee* was a Donzi eighty foot Tournament Sport Fishing Boat. The biggest charter boat on the Outer Banks. Only head boats were larger. But head boats were the least fun you could have on the water. Sixty people trying to catch one fish. The Donzi had a master stateroom, two smaller staterooms, Captain's quarters and room for a crew of three. Three heads. Full galley. Forty-three hundred dollars for the two day, one night trip. Plus tips for the crew. Food included. Booze not.

Since Oden's only had about thirty berths—boat parking spaces, Ken—it was a safe bet.

"Let me grab my stuff," Ken called, polishing off his sandwich and throwing his coffee cup away. His "stuff" was a wheeled carry-on size piece of luggage that appeared to be crammed full. Cutter suspected Ken had three changes of clothes, and a full bar, in there.

"Here. Hold this." Ken shoved his bag at Cutter. "I've got to get some suntan lotion."

No shit. Ken's complexion could only be described, on his good days, as pasty. Elmer's glue pasty—white, with a shine. Reminded Cutter of the belly of a frog. There was not going to be enough sunscreen or SPF shirts to keep him from being a crispy critter by sundown.

His mousy hair and skinny frame, along with the

pasty skin, screamed, "Dork!!!!" Even his expensive wardrobe could not help. His looks and his penchant for being an irritant successfully masked what was, it turned out, a first-rate ability to lawyer. Especially when it came to negotiations. Plus a loyalty that was dogged.

Five minutes later, Ken emerged from the ship's store with a huge tube of sunscreen and a Hatteras fishing cap on his head, the kind with the twelve inch bill in front and the drop down curtain in the back to protect the neck. Along with his Orvis shirt, his plaid shorts and his never-worn-before topsiders, he was the picture of the true deep sea fisherman.

Cutter had spied the *Debbie Lee* at the end of the line of charter boats, most of which were busy loading bait and drinks and other pasty, would-be Ahabs. As he and Ken neared the *Debbie Lee*, Cutter felt a little self-conscious. This boat was at least three times as large as any of the others. Just the kind of ostentatious display he would expect, not from Clint, but from Clint's wife, Lynn. Good thing the folks back home couldn't see this.

"Permission to come aboard, sir." Ken, the sailor, had been studying his naval law.

The black kid on the deck, who was busy shoveling ice into a hole in the floor, looked up, looked around to see who Ken was talking to and, since he was the only one there, answered, "Yeah. Sure. Come on board. Watch your step though," looked at Cutter and shook his head.

"Hi. I'm Ken. This is my friend Cutter," extending his hand.

"Hey. I'm Jordair. I'm the mate. I'll get the captain for you."

The rest of the group had not yet arrived. No surprise. They weren't late, however. Whenever Clint arrived, that was on time. After that was late. Since this outing was about mayoral business, and since Clint was the mayor, it would operate on Clint time.

Clinton Colin Brandsgard. Mayor of the City of Davenport. State of Iowa. Used to be called Zeke, but decided that wasn't formal enough. Thirty-five years old. Smart. Handsome. Charming. Described by the local press as a "rising star in politics."

Mayor Brandsgard had arranged for his inner circle to vacation together at the Outer Banks so he could get them on this boat for thirty-six hours to, as he put it, "plan our reelection campaign and map out our collective future." That was the royal "our".

In addition to Ken and Cutter this inner circle included Patrick Kovachik, the mayor's campaign manager and recently resigned chief of staff. Pat was the gray hair of the group. Quiet, sharp and reputedly had, after getting down on all fours, gotten a junk yard dog to whimper and turn tail. A hungry, irritable junk yard dog. No one really believed it had happened. But no one yet had tested the hypothesis that it was not true. Finally there was Sandy Morton, Clint's Education and Human Services Director. She brought a heart to the group. And a terrifying ability to see through bullshit. She also looked really good on camera, standing there behind the mayor when he announced his newest initiative, which invariably, Sandy had devised.

Cutter handled PR for the administration. Speech writing. Position papers. He was also the closest thing to a friend that Clint had in the group, though Ken thought of himself as a friend as well. One who just happened to be able to handle the mayor's personal legal matters...conveniently.

Completing the entourage was the First Lady of Davenport, Lynn Brandsgard. She was abided by the others. But barely.

"Hey, troops." The mayor's campaign voice bellowed down the dock. Clint was beaming, taking huge strides toward the *Debbie Lee*, leaving the rest of the group in his wake. With the rising sun behind him, he looked—and Cutter was sure he knew he looked—like the Second Coming.

"Isn't this great? What a terrific day." Over his shoulder, "Come on, Pat. Sandy. The guys are waiting. Hey, Cutman, you ready to catch some fish? Kenny, my man!"

Christ in a handbasket. This was gonna be a long thirty-six hours.

Walking slowly behind the mayor was Pat, and behind him, Lynn and Sandy in conversation. Sandy was wearing shorts and a tee shirt with a backpack over her shoulder. Lynn had on designer capris, designer shirt, designer boat shoes and carried a Longchamps purse. Just the outfit to take fifty miles out into the Atlantic to attract a marlin.

Behind the two women was a young man burdened with a gym bag for Clint, a small suitcase for Pat and two large suitcases for Milady. Cutter and Ken sat on the gunwales and waited for the rest to board.

Behind them quietly stood T. Jefferson, skipper (and owner) of the *Debbie Lee*. Tall and thin with features that years earlier had been called chiseled. Now they were just stone that had been eroded by forty years of sun and sand and wind and sea. A countenance not to be fucked with.

In the quietest of voices, the kind of quiet that made both Cutter and Ken jump, the captain ordered, "Jordair. Sam. Chop-chop. Help these people with their gear, please."

Cutter and Ken both wheeled toward the voice, Ken jumped up and stuck out his hand.

"Ken Riley, sir. Pleased to meet you."

"Tom Jefferson." Captain Jefferson took the proffered hand into both of his large weather-beaten hands and held it firmly. "The pleasure is mine." He shook Ken's hand once and slowly released it.

The normally motor-mouthed Ken was oddly speechless.

The captain turned to Cutter. "Tom Jefferson," and offered his hand. Cutter took it, they shook and Cutter grinned.

Jefferson turned his attention to the arriving guest and moved to the gangplank. As the mayor stepped aboard, the captain, by now with his hands tucked behind him in a military at-ease posture, welcomed them aboard.

"Welcome to the *Debbie Lee*. I am your captain, Tom Jefferson, and this is Jordair and Samantha, your mates, cooks and guides for our trip." Cutter wondered why the captain had suddenly changed from the friendly to the point of confidential to the formal. Ken remained speechless.

The rest followed Clint onto the *Debbie Lee*.

"Jordair and Sam will help you stow your gear below decks. Then we'll take a brief tour of the boat and review some safety information. I do thank you for choosing us for your outing, and if there is anything any of us can do to make your trip more enjoyable, please do not hesitate to ask." Captain Jefferson finished his boarding litany.

The young man with all the luggage stood at the bottom of the gangplank looking lost. Lynn turned back toward him and snapped, "Well, don't just stand there, looking like a dolt. Bring my bags up here so this boy can take them to our suite."

Cutter saw the barely concealed flash of anger pass across Clint's face. But almost instantaneously Clint replaced it with his mayoral grin and said, "Never mind, son, just set them down right there," and he strode back down the gangplank. "I'll take them myself," and pressed a twenty dollar bill into the kid's hand. "Thanks for all your help. You have a terrific day."

With that Clint picked up all four bags and climbed back aboard. Turning toward Jordair, he said, "Please show me the way, my good man." Smiling. And shooting the ole stink eye at his wife.

She missed it. Everyone else, including Jordair, did not. It had its intended effect. Jordair smiled at him and thought, "Boy! my ass."

Christ in a hand basket. The thirty-six hours just kept getting longer.

With Samantha leading the way and Ken right on her heels, trying to chat her up, the party lined up and went below deck to their cabins.

As they entered the very well-appointed stateroom, Lynn turned sharply at the door and huffed, "Excuse me, but the mayor and I are supposed to have the big cabin."

Samantha replied, "Ma'am, this is the master stateroom, the largest and nicest on the *Debbie Lee*. It has its own head, uh, bathroom, and I'm sure you will find it quite comfortable."

"Kinda small," was all Lynn could say.

Cutter and Ken shared a cabin. Pat, who suffered from sleep apnea and had to get hooked up to a Continuous Positive Airway Pressure (CPAP for short) machine every night, had his own cabin. Well, that, and Pat really didn't want to go on this adventure— "C'mon, Clint, I have much more important matters I need to be dealing with"—so he was getting preferential treatment.

They were one stateroom short so Samantha had agreed to let Sandy share her quarters. As the others settled in and stowed their belongings, Samantha showed Sandy to her small cabin in the stern.

Sandy apologized, "I really hope I'm not putting you out, Samantha."

"Oh, no problem, ma'am. It will be nice to have the company."

"Please, call me Sandy. Ma'am is my mother. Oh, and the mayor's wife."

"Okay, Sandy, thanks. You want the top bunk or the bottom?" she asked. She noticed Sandy looked a little green around the gills. "Are you alright? Do you get seasick?"

"I don't think so. I'm just feeling a bit queasy," Sandy said. The boat was barely rocking at all.

"Maybe you should be wearing a patch. I'll get you one," and Samantha left the cabin.

"Damnation. I hope I don't puke," thought Sandy and she lay down on the lower bunk. Thirty seconds later she was in the head, losing her breakfast but clearing her head. She felt one hundred per cent better. Or at least seventy-five percent.

Jordair tapped lightly on each cabin door and announced, "Ten minutes, on deck, please."

Twenty minutes later everyone was assembled in front of Captain Jefferson. Everyone except Lynn.

"I'm sorry," Jefferson said, "but where is Mrs. Brandsgard? We can't start until everyone is here."

Clint apologized, "Lynn has developed a headache and needed to lie down. I can share the information with her later."

"I'm sorry," Jefferson said, "but regulations require me to share this information with everyone on board before we leave the dock. Please have her join us."

Three minutes later everyone, including a pouting Lynn, was on deck.

Captain Jefferson welcomed them a second time, explained they would be going out about fifty miles into the Gulf Stream where "the big ones are" and that fair weather was predicted for the entire trip. He pointed out all of the safety features and ran through basic operational procedures. He closed with a final word.

"We are here to make some great memories for you. Understand, please, once a craft leaves dock, the captain's orders are the law. In the case of the *Debbie Lee* that includes the orders of the staff. Do you all understand and agree?"

They all nodded and voiced their assent, including a hearty, "Aye-aye, sir," from Ken and an, "I guess," from the still irked Lynn.

Captain Jefferson nodded at Jordair who jumped onto the dock and started releasing the mooring lines. The captain climbed aloft to the pilot's chair, started the throaty engines and did a final instrument check. Radioed the dock master and slowly slid the *Debbie Lee* into the channel.

After he finished securing the lines, Jordair found

the men—the women had already retreated to their cabins—and explained, "We are going to head out about seven miles, and we'll do a little trolling. Maybe catch a few Spanish mackerel or a sea bass which Samantha can prepare for lunch. Make yourselves comfortable. I'll rig up some poles. When we cross over from the sound to the ocean, it will be a little bumpy, but it'll be smooth sailing from there."

Pat found a table and a seat in the shade where he opened his lap top and shut out the rest of the world. Ken went in search of Samantha to "get a cup of coffee", trying to justify his pursuit. Clint followed Jordair to look at all the fishing gear and bug him with questions. Leaving Cutter to explore the boat. He wandered to the bow, holding on and trying to get his sea legs, went atop to watch the captain pilot the boat (which appeared to him to be just sitting in a nice chair, hands on the wheel, practicing the thousand-yard stare) and down below deck where he found the dining room and the galley and a small den like room which contained books and charts and nautical looking instruments.

And Sandy. Who was crying.

THREE

Why the hell had he ever taken this job? It bored him silly, the people were monotonous and the pay was for crap. Cutter sat at his desk, bouncing his pen on the tablet like a drum stick on a snare drum and moaned. Christ in a hand basket.

He'd been hired by the Humane Society Board to help a new NGO CEO—he was getting pretty good with the initializing of his life, like BFD for big deal and RFN for right now, though his mother didn't think much of his Yule greeting of MFC. He'd been hired to "solidify the CEO's thoughts on leadership." Whatever the fuck that meant. The CEO, George Gentry, didn't seem to have a clue. George was, by training and temperament, an accountant who became CEO because he was the last man standing after his predecessor almost bankrupted the organization, a shelter which saved and then found families for unwanted pets. Sometimes they found homes. Mostly, there weren't enough homes to go around. What the organization really did, and for some reason no one on the staff or the board seemed to accept the fact, was kill unwanted pets. Nasty business.

The Board figured what they needed now was a CEO with a head for business. What they got was a man who had been successful by keeping his door closed and his nose in a spreadsheet. If the only tool a person has is a hammer, well, then every problem looks like a nail. So old George changed his title, closed his door and stuck his nose in a spreadsheet, hoping it would work.

It didn't. The financial bleeding stopped but the staff members were soon at each other's throats.

The Board hired Cutter because one of the board members was also on the lait board at St. Mary of the Light and remembered how well Cutter had handled his work with the staff there. That and the Board was, by now, desperate.

As was Cutter. The whole have-to-pay-the-rent thing. Cutter had no idea where to start. What was it that Inigo had told Fezzik? Go back to the beginning. Back to the beginning.

The six rules. The rules he and his brothers and sisters had been taught. His parents thought with all those kids, it would be easier to teach them a few rules than to spend all of their parenting time as adjudicators and referees. Those rules were in order:

1. Don't get hurt.
2. Don't forget the first rule.
3. Take care of your brothers and sisters.
4. Treat people like you want them to treat you.
5. Grandpa's rule—have fun.
6. Don't take things that don't belong to you.

There had been a seventh rule—If it is your cousin Patrick's idea, it is probably not a good one—but that didn't seem to apply here.

As Cutter was mulling how to make the rules into George's mantra for staff cooperation, his phone rang.

"Yes?"

"Mr. Cutter, y'all have a call on line two," drawled Miss Perkins, the office southern belle and busybody. It had taken Cutter several days to figure out that "y'all" was one person—more than one was "all y'all".

"Okay." He waited for the call to come through.

"Hello?"

"Mr. Williams?"

"Yes."

"This is Rose Mary Denton. From Our Lady. We worked together a couple of months ago."

"Sure. Hey Rose Mary, how's it going? How's that, uh, Fenton, doing?"

"He's the same. But I'm calling about Amanda. She's having some problems and I know you liked her and I thought maybe you could help her."

"Sure. What's the problem?"

"She's pregnant. And unmarried. And Mr. Fenton is going to fire her."

Cutter took the handset away from his ear. Held it in front of his face and stared through it. So that had been it. Of course she didn't want to go out with him. She was boned, apparently both literally and figuratively. And that fucking Fenton had just been waiting for an opportunity for payback.

24

"Mr. Williams? Mr. Williams? Cutter?" Cutter heard a tiny voice that sounded far away. Realized he was looking at it. Put the phone back to his ear.

"Sorry. So Amanda asked you to call me?"

"Oh, no. She doesn't know. But someone has to help her, and I didn't know who else to call," Rose Mary explained.

"How do you think I can help? Fenton sure wouldn't listen to me. In fact, I would be more hurt than help. And I didn't really know anyone at the Diocese."

Rose Mary sounded disappointed. "Well, I don't know. I thought maybe there was something legal or something. Can they just fire her? That doesn't seem right."

Cutter thought about it. Ironic, really. Had she chosen an abortion, a choice the Church could condemn, no one would have been the wiser.

"So what is Amanda's plan? Do you know?" Cutter asked.

"She said she is going to have the baby and give it up for adoption," said Rosemary.

"What about the father? Won't he help? Or the adopting parents?" Cutter didn't like the sound of this or where it might end up.

Rose Mary sighed. "I really don't know. Amanda isn't saying much. I just couldn't think of anyone else to call. I'm sorry I bothered you."

Oh great, laying on the guilt. The classic Catholic ploy.

Now it was Cutter's turn to sigh. "I'll call her, Rose Mary. See if there's anything I can do."

"Well, please don't tell her I called you. Please."

She hung up. Cutter went back to staring at the rules he had written down. Shit. Number 3. And Number 4. No choice. He had to see if he could help. But after he figured out a way to make old George into the Mother Teresa of the humane society world.

Much rather be sitting on the deck of the Boat House Restaurant, drinking a beer and watching the barges on the Mississippi grind up river. Especially on this first warm day in March.

Screw it. He buzzed Miss Perkins. "Ma'am, I have to leave. Tell Mr. Gentry I'll be in early tomorrow."

"Y'all have a nice evening." Lord help us.

Cutter was waiting for his beer when he called Amanda.

"Hello?"

Cutter tried his nonchalant voice, "Hey, Amanda, this is Cutter Williams. From the school a couple months ago?"

"Oh, yeah. Hi, Cutter," a note of recognition in her voice.

Cutter jumped in, "I hate to bother you, but I have a HUGE favor to ask."

"What?" guarded.

Cutter explained what he was working on, told her about dull old George and about how it might be impossible to get old George from Point A to Point B.

"So, the thing is, I was pretty impressed with the

way the other teachers at St. Mary of the Tight Ass seemed to follow your lead and I thought maybe if I could bounce a few ideas off you, I might be able to come up with something that would work for old George. Or you might."

He realized he sounded lame.

"Depends," she said, "will you tell me the real story of how you got your name?"

Cutter smiled. "If you're not doing anything now, I'm at the Boat House. Come on down and I'll buy you a burger and a beer."

"If you can wait thirty minutes, I can do that."

"Sure. Ta-ta. Cheerio, mum."

"Oh, and no more of your crappy English accent," she demanded. "See you in thirty."

By now, Cutter was grinning. He'd forgotten how much he liked talking to her.

When she arrived forty-five minutes later, Cutter was on his third beer. He'd been contemplating how on TV or in the movies when a guy—a tough guy detective or a dusty cowboy or a battled-hardened soldier—walked into a bar and the bartender said, "What'll it be?" the guy would say "gimme a beer" and a beer—a mug or a bottle—would appear. No decisions, just a beer. At any bar in the Quad Cities you had to make five choices (IPA or lager? Bottle or draft? Iced mug or not? Short or tall? You want cherries and whipped cream on that?) just to get the goddamn beer. Bet over in Iowa City, you could just order a beer. College towns made it easier. Cutter spent a lot of time thinking philosophical thoughts.

"Hey, Winnie," she called across the deck. She looked great. She'd gotten her brown hair cut into kind of a shag. Five feet two inches tall, maybe a hundred and ten pounds soaking wet, great butt and boobs that were a little larger than when he last saw her. She had big eyes, a wide mouth and looked like what Sally Fields might have looked like if she were as pretty as Amanda. She didn't, to Cutter's eye, look pregnant.

She sat down, "I'm famished." Cutter soon learned that Amanda had four states of existence. "Hungry." "Starved." "Famished." Or "Eating." She waved a waitress over. Ordered a cheeseburger—well done for the baby, though she preferred almost raw—fries and a chocolate milkshake. She ignored Cutter's raised eyebrows at the milkshake order.

"So, Mr. Bullshit, why did you really call me? Won't take 'no' for an answer?"

Cutter stammered "Uh, no, really, I could use your help. You see, this job is…yeah, ok, bullshit. I just wanted to see you."

They spent the next two hours eating, drinking—her milkshakes, plural; him—beer, plural; and talking. About that fucking Fenton and the other teachers. About the Humane Society (she thought it was great that he was helping those poor animals). About her family, small and formal. His family, large and chaotic. About movies and books.

"So you want to go out Saturday? Dinner?" he asked.

"I can't." Her eyes welled up.

28

"Christ, what did I say wrong?"

"Nothing. I'm sorry, Cutter, it's not that...I can't. I'm pregnant."

Cutter looked at her. "So?"

"So? What the fuck do you mean 'so'?" she demanded, her voice a little too loud.

"So what does that have to do with dinner? Pregnant girls don't eat?" he wondered.

Amanda stared at him. And then told him about dating Terry for three years. And breaking up and it breaking her heart. How he had been the one. How she had tried to fill the void by dating, too seriously, other men. How the rhythm and blues birth control method had failed her. How she really didn't believe in abortion. How it was going to cost her her job. And by the time she was finished, there were no tears. Only firmly fixed eyes and a set jaw.

Cutter smiled and asked, "You wanna have dinner Saturday? How about the Faithful Pilot?"

Finally, she said "Yes." Finally.

Cutter asked her about losing her job.

"They told me. Actually, your friend Dr. Fenton told me that it was a moral infraction. Whatever that is. And that I would have to leave by the fifth month. That's in about eight weeks. Terminated. No Pay. No going away gift. No watch."

"Geez, Amanda, that doesn't seem fair. Have you talked to a lawyer?"

She had. Plus a women's rights organization. Nothing of any help.

"What about the father?"

Out of the picture, never in the picture. He'd been told and sent packing. No help sought, no help offered.

"Parents?"

"Oh god, I can't even bring myself to tell them. This will kill them. Not because of what I'm going through but because of what their friends will think." Amanda was clearly shaken by this.

She stood abruptly. "I have to go. I'll see you Saturday. Call me. And sorry about all this. Thanks for listening."

"No problem," he said. He watched as she walked away, thinking she looked as good going as she did coming.

What the fuck was he thinking?

FOUR

Ken was sweating like a frosty mug on a humid day—and the sun was already burning through his ample application of sunscreen. Nonetheless, he was smiling. He was holding on to a fishing rod which was bent forty-five degrees toward the ocean surface. He alternately reeled and pulled the rod upward just like Jordair had shown him. Ken had completed his transition from super sailor to super angler.

"Not too fast. Not too fast. Slow. That's it. Let him run when he wants. He'll get tired. You're smarter than this fish. You own him," Jordair encouraged.

"You forget Ken's a lawyer—he may not be that much smarter," Cutter offered. Jordair laughed.

"Come on, Kenny. You can do it," Clint encouraged.

"Must be really big. What do you think it is?" asked Pat. Even he had gotten caught up in the moment.

The *Debbie Lee* had a real *bona fide* fishing chair—just like Hemingway's. Okay, so maybe this one had a padded seat and arm rests, a shoulder harness and

31

places for a beer and your cell phone, but still it was a place to become a man by hauling in a swordfish or a marlin.

Now, however, they were fishing shallow water and Ken was standing, knees locked, shoulders straining at the stern. He was as excited as Cutter had ever seen him.

"Maybe a false albacore. Fighting lots, though. Maybe a big blue. Might even be a scrod," Jordair answered Pat.

"What's scrod?" Ken wanted to know.

Deadpan from Jordair, "The pluperfect subjunctive. Screw, screwed, scrod." Only the English major laughed.

They had started the trip with Bloody Marys—Pat and Sandy just orange juice—but everyone else had two—and Lynn, three. They all agreed Samantha made the best ever. Ken, of course, had to argue that the best Bloody Mary was from the Eleven City Diner in Chicago, but the others hooted him down and, in a moment of clarity—and chagrin—Ken realized he'd just lost points with Samantha. Damn.

They were a couple of hours into their adventure. So far, it was a lot better than Cutter had imagined. He had stumbled into Sandy crying, but it turned out it was, according to her, sea sickness, stress and missing Paul, her asshole husband. Asshole as far as Cutter was concerned. Barrel-chested, testosterone laden, Iowa State wrestler, tight-ass moneyman, Paul. But that was just Cutter's opinion. He knew you didn't fuck with

Paul. Paul was bagman and fixer for Gerald Huntsman, the Quad Cities number one Titan. The CEOs of all the banks, hell, the CEO of Ramrod Industrial Machinery, Iowa's biggest manufacturer, all checked in with Jerry before they did anything. The local newspaper never ran an editorial that Jerry didn't see first. Not that Jerry didn't have the community's best interest at heart. You just didn't cross him.

Legend had it that Jimmy Carter had gotten down on his knees and prayed in Jerry's office, asking God for Jerry's support. Tracy Rogers, up and coming political star, had decided he didn't need Jerry's support—that, in fact, Jerry had far too much power in the community. Last anyone heard, Tracy was still serving a six year sentence for tax evasion. Still proclaiming his innocence. That he had been framed. That he couldn't explain that money in his account. That someone else had put it there. But then, jails are full of innocent people. Or so they say.

It was almost ordained that at some point the paths of Gerald Huntsman and Clinton Colin Brandsgard would cross. When Clint was in college at Augustana, he looked across the Mississippi from his dorm room at his hometown and decided in a flash of predestination that he wanted to be the President of the United States. And why not? He was smart enough, he had the looks and he had the charisma. What he didn't have was the money or the contacts. What he needed was a plan to get those things.

So he worked backwards, from the Presidency to

his current position of college student. Presidents rose through the ranks of a few select professions—occasionally a general or college professor snuck in, but those professions could be eliminated—leaving Congressman (too many competitors), Senator (still ninety-nine competitors) or Governor. Much better. Only fifty of those.

So governor of Iowa it was. Good state to make the jump from. Small enough that a person could get elected and a place where you could jump start a campaign with favorite son status in the presidential caucuses.

Quickest road to the Governor's Mansion? Be the mayor of a big city. Davenport mayor it would be. How do you become mayor? First become a member of City Council. Where could you make the contacts to make a run for Council? Easiest place would be the Chamber of Commerce. A job there would pay you to develop those contacts.

Clinton Colin Brandsgard changed his major the next day from pre-law, though his roomie Ken Riley told him it was a stupid thing to do, to Business Communication.

Not surprisingly, his plan worked. Six years later he was Vice President for Business Development at the Chamber, a position that introduced him to Paul Morton, bagman for the king maker, who introduced him to Jerry Huntsman, the king maker himself. Mr. Huntsman agreed to support Clint's run for council and sent him to Patrick Kovachik, who Huntsman thought could handle this brash kid.

The rest was, as they say, history. He was now thirty-five years old, in his fourth year as mayor and kicking off his re-election campaign. Not that he hadn't been a good mayor. In fact, he was highly regarded and was making Davenport THE place to live and work. In spite of itself.

His major breakthrough was almost a fluke. At a business luncheon, Mr. Huntsman was bemoaning the fact that many of the young smart people were leaving and not coming back. And that because the education system was at best second rate, things were not likely to change. Clint thought little of it—after all, the schools were under a separate school board and politically, public education was quicksand. Most who went in never came back.

But later that week, at yet another cocktail party for yet another public art unveiling, the subject came up in a conversation Clint had with Paul. Paul was bitching that his boys were really pissed at the School Board and wanted them all kicked out, which meant a lot of work for Paul.

Paul's wife Sandy stood quietly listening to the conversation. Clint turned to her and asked, "What do you think?"

"I don't understand. What do I think about what?"

Clint tried again, "What do you think of the idea of getting rid of all the School Board members and starting over? Would that help?"

Sandy wasn't sure he really wanted her opinion.

35

She had seen this young mayor in action and thought he was mostly just about the politics. But she'd been asked and, in fact, she did have an opinion—a strong one. She pulled over a soap box and climbed up.

"You see all this," Sandy waved her arms around at the art opening. "We spend millions of dollars a year on museums and art and farmers' markets and fireworks and bridges to nowhere. All from the city's share of the casino taxes. All because a small group of old men think tourist attractions will attract families and business. And because one old biddy loves to stand up," she pointed at a gray-haired matron holding court across the room, "and be applauded." Sandy finally took a breath.

"And?" Clint went on.

"Go to the State legislature, convince them to give that money to the City for educational purposes. Paul could help with the legislature. Then use the money to set up a scholarship fund for graduates of Davenport schools and for teachers in Davenport schools. Only open to residents of Davenport. Free college tuition. Parents will stream into the city. Property values will increase. Business will follow. More funding for education. You control the money into and out of the scholarship fund. The school district will have to listen to you."

Clint hired her on the spot.

Two and a half years later, elected officials were coming from all over to study what Davenport had done.

Clint was already looking past the mayor's race—that was *a fait accompli*—and eyeing the governor's race two years out. Gerald Huntsman was beaming like a new father. He knew he had a horse he could ride to the top. Since Jerry was happy, his bagman was happy, though he didn't like the amount of time his wife spent at City Hall.

The mayor's wife? Well, she was damned near ecstatic. The more famous her husband became, the more she got invited to dinners and parties and chances to rub elbows with the rich and the more famous. The mayor's salary wasn't much but the campaign fund always seemed to be able to buy, and equally importantly justify buying, her new clothes, new furniture and a new BMW.

Pat was happy. He not only had a candidate who was electable, but one who was malleable. If he told Clint to do this or that, Clint did it. Clint was a bankable asset—no problem fund raising. Plus in his position as chief of staff, Clint let him make whatever political appointments he deemed necessary. Sometimes Pat closed his door, closed his eyes and thought about the West Wing.

Ken was happy. His college friend had made life interesting. Most of his life was just routine work at the firm but being around Clint added some spice. Though not always good. Like having to cover for Clint's dalliance with the lady vice president at the bank. Their affair was heated and mutually exciting, right up to when Clint's eye roved again. She had demanded money, which Jerry put up, after a stern warning to Clint about his little soldier going AWOL again. But Ken had to draw up the contract to insure that for now and forever, this would remain quiet. To make up for it, there were the political events, the parties, the contacts. Mostly it was that this important man actually looked to Ken for advice. Ken, in fact, had been the one who sat down and negotiated with the School Board to extract the Memo of Understanding which gave the mayor *de facto* authority over the Superintendent which led to Ken's negotiating the severance package for the Superintendent, who apparently did not like his new boss. Not surprisingly, it was Kenneth Riley who was chosen to lead the search committee for a new superintendent.

Sandy was happy. Finally someone—Clint—listened to her. She loved Paul, but she always had the feeling that he and his boss and his job were more important to him than she was. She was pretty sure her ideas and suggestions never went further than in one of Paul's ears and out the other. She had been right about the education thing. Sure, it took Clint's position and Huntsman's money, but she was the one who developed the concept. Put in the extra hours every week to make it work. She didn't get the recognition outside the group. But she knew. She also knew there was more, much more, to come.

Cutter had been the last one to the party. Sandy had been making the rounds to the community's schools—public and private—and ran into several teachers and administrators (not including that fucking Fenton) who suggested she look him up. Seems he had a flair for working with teachers. She Googled him. His career, if you could call it that, was sketchy. Mostly consulting piecework. The picture she patched together was almost abstract—good with staff, empathetic, prick to by-the-book administrators, good writer, able to help people find common ground, apolitical, didn't care a whit about his appearance. And, most oddly, the Catholic Bishop seemed to have a real fondness for him.

"Mr. Williams?" Sandy asked into the phone.

"Yes?"

"My name is Sandy Morton. I work with Clint Brandsgard."

"Who?"

"Clint Brandsgard, the Mayor of Davenport." God, this guy was beyond apolitical. He was oblivious.

"Oh. Yeah. Hi. What can I do for you?"

"Have lunch with me," she replied.

"You buying?" he asked. Before she could assure him that, yes indeed, she was buying, he added, "No. Wait. I'm not sure I want the Mayor buying me lunch. That sounds a little dangerous."

"It won't be," Sandy replied. "The Boat House? Tomorrow at noon?"

She was startled how quickly his reply came, "No, not the Boat House. I don't go there. How about someplace in the East Village?"

"The 11th Street Precinct?"

"Fine. See you there tomorrow."

"Thank you. See you then," she said and started to hang up.

"Uh, Ms. Morton?"

"Yes?"

"How will I know you?" Wow, this guy really was oblivious. What to tell him? Geez, guy, look for the woman who has been in the paper or on TV about fifty times, standing behind the mayor.

"I'll have a red rose between my teeth," she said instead.

He thought he might like her. And the smile showed through the phone. "Great. I'll be wearing tights and a cape. See you then," and he hung up.

He did like her—immediately. He showed up five minutes early, carrying a red rose. She walked over to him and handed him a mug of beer. He didn't even have to decide what kind. What was not to like? She was terrific looking. Funny. Smart. Married. Though he thought of that as a temporary affliction. Most importantly, she had something he needed. A job.

While they waited for their food—here in the East Village it would be German—Sandy got down to business.

"Winston, we think…"

He cut her off. "Could you call me Cutter?"

"Okay, Cutter. We think what we are doing is very, very important. And that you could help us."

Sandy explained about how the legislature had agreed to funnel gambling funds into their project

40

(Lord, did this guy never read the paper?) And that they were setting up the scholarship fund but needed help with school districts buying in and with writing the position papers and speeches.

Cutter looked around the room. Cooler after cooler, tap after tap of beers. Must be two hundred fifty different kinds. Christ, it's just beer. Thought about his grandfather who claimed that he was a "common sewer of beer" and had belly-laughed at his own play on words. Grandpa would have shit his pants looking at this place. So how to play this. Negatives: It's politics. Nasty fucking business. Though they aren't killing cats and dogs or selling used cars. Yet. But it is a job. And this girl is something. And maybe could become something.

"Okay," he answered. "But understand, I can't lie about things," thinking about what he believed of politicians. Then he thought about that fucking Fenton. "Unless I believe lying is important."

Three days later, wearing a tie he found at his parents' home—they were so excited that he was meeting with the mayor—he met with Clint Brandsgard. Whom he liked. A lot. And he accepted a job. With benefits.

To celebrate, he bought a suit and got a haircut.
And got drunk.

FIVE

It was the kind of evening that made you believe winter was just a memory, even though it was still March. Seventy-five degrees. Absolutely balmy on the Mississippi.

"Really nice out," Cutter said as they walked up the cobblestone street toward the Faithful Pilot.

"Then you should keep it out," Amanda responded. It broke his stride. She was twenty feet ahead of him before he could start moving again.

"Thanks. I will," he yelled at her back. She almost turned around to see if he was serious. Decided she didn't really want to know.

After they ordered dinner, which was after she had to explain to him why she couldn't drink alcohol (pregnancy and babies were not something he had given much thought to—in fact, no thought to at all would be more accurate), they sat for a while without talking, just looking out the window at the river. It was still running high from the snow melt up in Minnesota but nowhere near flood level.

"I've been thinking about your job problem." Actually it was all he had been thinking about, but he sure didn't want to share that with her.

"Yeah?" she wondered.

"I have an idea. Something I would be willing to do—in fact, very happy to do—though it probably wouldn't work. Sort of a last ditch effort. Also it depends on how you feel about Fenton. I want to make him…" Cutter tried to turn his voice deep Sicilian, "an offer he can't refuse."

She smiled. Then she grinned. "Tell me."

He told her. She wasn't sure. But she was getting a little desperate. She had talked to the adoption agency, thinking that maybe the adopting parents could help out a little financially. She had been told while it was expected they would cover the medical expenses, it would be illegal to pay her anything. On account of avoiding the appearance of selling babies. Shit.

Reluctantly, she agreed to Cutter's plan. They ate and talked. She asked again about his name. He told her he would tell her sometime. They finished, drove back to the Quad Cities, stopped at Whitey's for ice cream and he drove her home. She wouldn't let him get out of the car.

The following Tuesday, Amanda called off sick. At 10:30, Cutter arrived at St. Mary of the Light and asked to see Dr. Fenton. His receptionist was more than a little surprised to see him.

"Do you have an appointment?" She knew he didn't.

"No, ma'am. But I think Principal Fenton would love to see me."

"May I tell him what it is concerning?" she asked.

"Sure," he replied. Smiled. Nothing more.

"Well?" she asked. Irritated.

"Deep subject," he offered.

She was clearly getting very pissed at him. He didn't care. In fact, it made him relax. "I'm sorry, but if you won't tell me what you want, I can't help you."

"I did tell you what I want," he replied.

"What?" A little too loudly.

"I want to see Principal Fenton," and he smiled his aw shucks smile.

She got up and stomped back into fucking Fenton's inner sanctum. "I'm sorry, Dr. Fenton," she began, "but Mr. Williams. You remember him. Cutter Williams? He would like to see you. I told him if he didn't have an appointment he couldn't, but he is quite insistent. Obnoxious, actually. May I ask him to just leave?"

"Please do," Fenton smirked.

Now the receptionist smiled. "Thank you, sir," and she turned to deliver the good news to Cutter.

She walked to the door. Unfortunately, it gave Fenton the time to recall Cutter seemed to have some "in" with the Bishop. Leastwise, that was Fenton's read on it. "Wait a minute," he said.

She turned. "Sir?"

"Tell him to wait. I'll be out in a few minutes."

"Are you sure, sir? I can get rid of him."

"No. No. Thanks. I'll deal with our Mr. Cutter Williams," he declared, standing to his full height and Marine bearing.

Five minutes later Cutter sat in an uncomfortable, by intent and design, chair in front of Principal Fenton's desk. Uncomfortable and six inches lower than Fenton's chair.

"What can I do for you?" Fenton demanded.

"I want to talk to you about Amanda Reagan," Cutter started.

Fenton held his hand up. "Sorry. It's against policy to discuss any personnel or personnel issues. Especially if the employee is not present. So, please..."

Cutter interrupted, "Look, Ed, I think maybe you should take a little sip out of the shut-the-fuck-up cup. I need for you to listen. Listen and not respond. Think about what you are going to do and say. You think you can do that?"

Fenton, "What?" Cutter could see the vein in his forehead and the red crawling up his white sidewalls.

Cutter went on, "Clearly we have a problem. Well, I don't. You do. And Amanda does. What has happened to her was obviously a mistake. What you are doing to her is clearly wrong."

Fenton interrupted, "The policy states..."

"Shut-the-fuck-up cup, Ed. Remember? It's wrong and you know it. She will have no income. No insurance. Nothing. So this is what you are going to do." Cutter was feeling brazen. Also, scared shitless. If this didn't work, Amanda would suffer and his stock with her would fall. Fuck it. Onward. Upward. Or downward as the case may be.

"This is what you can do. You can tell your board,

the diocese and the staff you are putting Amanda on a paid sabbatical, she will continue all pay and benefits, and she will return to her position next fall."

"Or what?" Fenton seethed.

"Or I am going to hold a press conference. You know how much the Church wants press conferences these days. I am going to explain that Miss Reagan made a terrible mistake but was willing to do the right thing and have this child and give it up for adoption. Now, however, she cannot do this because you are totally unwilling to give her paid leave and carry her insurance, as you would for a married mother. She is therefore forced, against her will, to have an abortion. I'm sure the Bishop will love this. What do you think?"

Fenton's eyes hooded down, "Get out of my office, asshole. And go fuck yourself."

"Your call." Cutter stood and turned toward the door. "See you in the papers...and on the six o'clock news."

Cutter was almost out of the building when Fenton's receptionist caught him. "Mr. Williams. Mr. Williams. Dr. Fenton would like to see you for one more minute. Please."

"No. Tell Fenton the press conference is at 11:00 tomorrow morning." Cutter turned and walked away. Though the morning was March windy and cold, he felt perspiration running down his back.

That night Dr. Edward T. Fenton called Amanda Reagan and made her an offer she could not refuse. He also told her that he hoped someday to repay Winston Williams for all his help. And that it might be for the best if she started her sabbatical the following week. Amanda wasn't happy about leaving her kids mid-year, but she agreed.

"How can I ever thank you?" she asked Cutter.

"Well…" he drew out the word. A smile that could only be called a leer.

"Forget it, buster. Ain't never gonna happen. Remember, I am in a delicate condition. Besides, you are not my type," she was smiling.

"What is your type?" he wondered.

"Well, right now, not male. I mean, not female either, but men are definitely not high on my list."

"How about us boys?" he asked.

"Didn't know there was a difference." She actually sounded dead serious.

They were having breakfast on Saturday morning. French toast for her, some disgusting looking glob that had eggs, potatoes, sausage gravy and other unidentifiable lumps for him.

"How can you do that to your body?" she asked, pointing her fork at his plate.

"Breakfast of Champions. So what are you going to do now? I mean besides the obvious." Now he pointed his fork at her abdomen.

"I don't know, Cutter. Take a class or two. Read. Work out. I'm just not sure. Probably worry and fret a lot."

"Then I know how you can repay me," he said.

She raised her eyebrows. She still was never sure of what might come out of his mouth. "How?"

"Come help me at the Humane Society. Volunteer. You can't believe how depressing it is. Maybe share some of your..." He wasn't sure what the word was.

"My what?" Eyebrows raised again.

"Élan. Fervor. Positivity. *Je ne sais quoi.* You know. C'mon. It'll be fun."

"I'll think about it."

A week later, with a stern warning from her doctor to stay away from where they kept the cats, Amanda showed up at the Humane Society.

Cutter had learned the organization's problems went a lot deeper than merely a leader who couldn't lead. Chief among those problems was how the jobs were compartmentalized. A few employees had the fun, rewarding job of adopting out pets, some did nothing but clean up pet shit and others had the even more debilitating job of killing defenseless animals. No surprise the staff was ready to wage war on itself.

Cutter decided to attack both fronts. Now that he had a backup who belonged to no internal camp, the attack could be simultaneous. He would concentrate on old George, who gladly, happily, as close to gleefully as it got, abdicated staff supervision and training to Cutter and Amanda. Amanda took on the cross training of the staff. They liked her. The only people who objected were those with the good job. But they didn't object too loudly or too long.

Over the next two months, the place changed. Amanda had started pet care training classes for animal adopters and three of the staff opened a small retail operation in-house for pet supplies which actually brought in a little more money. Cutter even got old George out of his office and meeting regularly with his employees. Where old George preached his rules for making the place work effectively: 1. Don't get hurt; 2. Don't forget the first rule; 3. Take care of your work mates; *et cetera, et cetera, et cetera.* Old George didn't really understand the rule thing at all, but it seemed to make Cutter happy and it kept the staff away from him. Perfect.

"So you going up to Dubuque for Easter?" Cutter asked Amanda, referring to her family's home.

"No." The kind of "No" that was meant to end the conversation. It didn't.

"No? Why not? Easter not a big deal with your family?" he wondered.

She knew he wouldn't quit asking. "Actually, it is a big deal at the Reagans. All the aunts and uncles and cousins. Mass. Easter egg hunt. Big dinner. But I'm not welcome this year."

"What? Why not?"

"I told my parents. About the baby. Mom cried. Dad tsked. They don't want my younger sister to know. Or anyone else for that matter. I am welcome to return after this 'unpleasantness' is over. With the understanding that it is never, never, ever to be mentioned." She had that look on her face—the one Cutter did not like at all. The one that combined anger and disappointment and fear.

"You're shitting me. I'm sorry. Doesn't seem like a very nice way to treat a daughter."

"I don't want to talk about it."

He shut up.

Thirty minutes later he called to her across the office. "Hey, Amanda." He had tried several nicknames with her—Amy, Mandy, even Henrietta—but she insisted he, and everyone else, use her proper name. "Why don't you come with me to my folks' for Easter? I'll bet the little kids will even let you hunt eggs with them."

Which they did. Being there with the nieces and nephews, looking for chocolate bunnies and jelly beans and plastic "treasure" eggs, it was the first time Cutter ever saw her completely relaxed and happy.

Cutter was playing a game of catch with a nephew when his brother Jim came over and said to him, "Nice girl. Too bad she's pregnant."

Yeah. Too bad.

Six months later there was a small article on page ten of the paper about how the director of the Humane Society had barricaded himself in his office after a fight broke out among his staff members. The police had to break down the door to get him out. He was now "sedated and resting comfortably" at an undisclosed location. By then Cutter was way beyond caring. Or even noticing.

SIX

Ken was sitting in the shade, drinking a beer, still smiling over his victory. It had indeed been a blue-fish, good-sized. By the time he muscled it to the boat and Jordair had gaffed it onto the deck, Ken's arms and back had been throbbing. But seeing that fish made it worthwhile. They had all decided, yes, you bet, Samantha should cook it up for lunch, and she dragged it down to the galley as soon as Jordair finished cleaning it.

Captain Jefferson told them sometimes blues would be running, that is, schools would be moving and feeding together though generally not this far out or this time of year. Still, if they wanted he would turn around and make a couple more passes. Every-one, save Lynn who had gone below deck to "read" (which everyone knew was to sleep off her fourth Bloody Mary) cheered the idea of another pass or two, even if it meant losing a couple of hours of big game fish time.

On the next run, Cutter caught a small blue which he released and Clint took over the chair. Two passes resulted in no hits and Clint got bored so he turned the chair over to Pat. By then Sandy had gone to her quarters to change into her bathing suit to do some sunning on the fore deck. Soon after, Clint left the fishing deck and wandered to where Sandy was sunning.

Cutter slid over by Jordair. "Interesting name, Jordair. I don't think I've ever heard it before."

"No one else ever has either. Been having to spell it for people all my life. It gets a lot of eye rolls. Folks assume it's one of those young black mothers making up a name thing," Jordair offered.

"But that isn't it?" Cutter asked.

"Well, sort of, maybe. 'Cept it wasn't my mom. My dad wanted a basketball star for a son. My older brother, Anthony—nice regular name—smart guy, working on his master's, but couldn't walk and chew gum at the same time. So my dad decided if I was a boy, I would be named Michael Jordan. My mom would have none of it. Said she'd run my dad out if he named me that. Two hours after I was born, my dad snuck down to the nurses' station and had the birth certificate finished, without telling mom. And this was the name he gave me," Jordair smiled.

"Geez, that's great," Cutter said.

"What about you? Your name isn't exactly out of the book of names, is it?"

"Oh, my real name is Winston. Like in Churchill. Cutter is just a nickname."

"How'd you get it?"

"Funny, you of all people would ask," Cutter answered. By now, Ken had moved closer, just in case Cutter would finally reveal how he really got the name.

"Well?" Jordair asked.

"When I was a kid about five years old, my grandfather took me, my brothers Chris and Tad and my sister Patti fishing. Cane poles. Bobbers. Nightcrawlers. Going after the big ones—blue gills. Grandpa showed us how to slice the worms up, put them on the hook and set the bobber. Chris and Tad seemed to like it. I thought it was pretty boring. Patti, all she wanted to do was play with the worms. Clean them off with a tissue and put them in a little match box she had, kind of a worm dollhouse. My grandfather looked over at her and said, 'Hey, you gonna fish or cut bait?' and Patti just made a face and stuck out her tongue at him. Not me. I didn't want to fish, so I yelled, 'I wanna cut bait. I wanna do that. I wanna be the cutter.' Grandpa thought that was pretty damn funny and from that point on he called me 'Cutter'. It just stuck."

Jordair laughed. Before Ken could call, "Bullshit," Samantha announced lunch was served.

Five minutes later the Brandsgard Administration brain trust was seated around the table, Captain Jefferson was heading the *Debbie Lee* out to the Gulf Stream, Jordair was setting up the sailfish rigs and Samantha served up the bluefish along with corn on the cob, fried potatoes, and peach cobbler for dessert.

None of them had eaten bluefish before. They weren't prepared for how strong it was. Ken would eat anything so he shoveled it in, talking between mouthsful about, "How great is this? I caught it only an hour ago and now we're eating it." Well, he and Pat, who had no taste buds left from years of smoking, were eating it. Everyone else was politely pushing it around their plates and agreeing how Samantha had done a great job of fixing it. Samantha had been around enough to know most wouldn't like it. That's why she made lots of corn and potatoes.

Lynn took one bite, made a face, spit it out and asked Samantha for something else. "Do you have a chicken salad sandwich, maybe?"

"No, but I got tuna fish. Will that do?"

"Oh, I suppose. Thank you. You are such a sweetie." Lynn was on her best behavior.

Two minutes later Samantha was back with a white bread, canned tuna, imitation mayonnaise sandwich. Lynn made another face. Which was pretty much what Samantha was going for.

They talked about the outing so far. Ken made a point to say, loudly enough for her to hear back in the galley, how terrific Samantha was. It was decided, more by mayoral proclamation than by group acclamation, that Sandy would have first shot at the chair when something was hooked. Sandy wasn't so sure but agreed. Based on what Captain Jefferson had told them, they were still about ninety minutes away from where they would be fishing.

Lynn rose, swirled her sarong with kind of a flourish and announced she was going on deck to sun and read.

54

"Hey, Babe, I thought we could spend an hour or so on business before we go out there," her husband said, "and I would really like you to be a part of it."

"Oh, Clinton, you know how I hate politics. You people go ahead," she replied.

"I insist," he told her, the gentleness gone from his voice.

"Oh for Christsake," Cutter interjected, "sit down, Lynn, so we can get this over with." The woman was sandpaper on his psyche.

She snorted. But she sat. And pouted.

Clint stood—smiling his campaign smile as he surveyed his team. "Well, people, this is it. Today is the first day of our campaign. I'm sure you all understand I'm talking about our campaign for governor."

Lynn finally smiled.

"Now we won't be talking about that. We'll let others, like the newspaper and the talk shows, do that for us. All we will talk about is Davenport and how important the city is to us. Remember, though, everything we do and say, every program Sandy designs, every speech Cutter writes, every donation Ken brings in, they all will be aimed at the governor's race in two years."

He had their attention. He continued, "And in the statehouse is where this incredible team belongs." He actually thought "Whitehouse" but managed not to say it. He knew he was going there but seriously doubted any of the group, save the requisite wife, would actually be going with him.

"Each and every one of you. The best and the brightest. Over the next couple of days, here and back on the island, I want our plan laid out, roles assigned and a schedule finished. Right people on the bus. Wrong people off. People in the right seats facing forward. So our bus driver, Mr. Kovachik here, can get us safely to our destination." Clint loved campaign metaphors.

"First, I want Pat to lay out overall strategy. This evening Sandy will go over our next big initiative, tomorrow Kenny will talk about expanding our corporate funding base and Cutter will talk about media relations and how he is going to get a haircut and a new suit. Everybody got it?"

Nods all around.

"Pat?" Clint turned over the floor.

Pat stood and faced them. He didn't smile. Fact was, the only time he ever smiled was when a big donor tried to make a joke. Or when a political opponent went down in flames. Only one of them was a genuine smile.

Pat thought of this group as Camelot. Clint was King Arthur. But not yet on the throne. He had some good knights around him and this Guinevere he would have to keep a rein on because she might eventually say the wrong thing at the wrong time. He was, of course, Merlin, the wise teacher and counselor who could, when necessary, work a little magic.

In his college days, Pat had gotten involved in campus politics. Not because he was particularly inter-

56

ested, but because Beth, big-boobed Beth from his history class, was very excited about campus races. He volunteered to help, thinking it might lead to those marvelous boobs. It didn't, but he discovered he loved the politics. Not liberal/conservative, Democrat/Republican politics. The politics of a campaign. Winning a vote. Losing a vote. He had found his calling.

Early on he heard a story about a group of Texas Democrats which was trying to unseat a very popular Republican office holder. Finally a young man in the back of the room shouted out, "Let's tell people he fucks pigs." Lots of laughter and someone yelled back, "We can't do that. It's not true." The young man responded, "Yeah. I know that. You know that. But let him deny it." The young man, according to the legend, was Lyndon Baines Johnson. Pat assumed the story was just an illustrative myth, but the message wasn't wasted on him.

He was an assistant campaign manager for a state representative candidate. His guy was getting trounced. He figured, "What the hell," and started circulating a rumor about how the opponent was secretly into child porn. Circulated as in, "I can't believe someone said that about our opponent. It just couldn't be true." The guy had once been in the seminary. A small city like Cedar Rapids. Everyone knew everyone. No one believed it. Didn't stop the guy from calling a press conference to deny it. In one day he went from eleven points up to five points down. Pat's candidate made no statement save in response to a reporter's question.

"There is no way my opponent could be involved.

No way. He is the most honorable man I know. No voter should give this vicious rumor a second thought." As in, don't get this tune stuck in your head. Nail in the coffin. Pat was rewarded with the party's next state senator race.

A race in a part of the state in which there were large numbers of Hispanic farm workers. The incumbent, whose wife happened to be Hispanic, had turned out huge numbers of new Hispanic voters and easily won the seat his first time out. The new senator then became a rising star in the statehouse.

Pat's strategy was to contact the pastor of the largest Hispanic congregation in the district with an offer. "You bring me five Hispanic clergymen who will, on the same Sunday, endorse my candidate, and I will make sure you get appointed to the State Farm Workers' Board when my candidate is elected." That appointment carried some power and a large salary, especially considering it only took a few hours each month.

Four weeks later the pastors made their endorsement of Pat's candidate. The incumbent and his campaign team went ballistic. Their in-the-pocket, guaranteed votes had suddenly evaporated. Or so they thought. The reelection campaign spent all of its time and most of its money trying to win back votes they had never lost. Which gave Pat's candidate the opening she needed.

Pat was now the party's Chosen One. A title he held for a few years. Until one of his trusted aides got caught with one hand in the till and the other in the candidate's wife's pants. From that point on, Pat caught a long series of losers. The party bosses even started calling for-sure losers, "Kovachik Specials." Not to his face of course. But he knew. He filled time in mid-level politically appointed positions. Like assistant city clerk in Davenport where he got reacquainted with a big time party donor, one Gerald Huntsman.

It was Huntsman who had sent Pat this golden boy, Clint Brandsgard, with instructions to tame him down, tune him up and teach him how to be a political candidate. The best gift a hack ever got.

Merlin spoke, "We have just one strategy. Don't fuck up." He was not smiling. And only Clint dared smile back at him. "I'm very serious here. No one can beat the mayor. Especially neither of the two opposition front runners. I've seen enough losers to know one or the other of them will be offered the chance to run merely as a payoff for long time loyalty."

"We will spend almost all of our time in City Hall. You'll hear later about this idea Sandy has which will certainly work on the city level, be even better at the state level and bring the state national attention. Nine to five, we'll be working on that along with picking up the trash, arresting the bad guys and paving the streets."

"We'll try to limit campaign appearances to evenings, weekends and early mornings. The message will be simple. Remind voters of how great the city is doing, largely due to Clint's tuition program, and to lay out the next big thing. We won't debate. Hell, we won't respond to anything the other candidate says. If that becomes absolutely necessary, Cutter will do a little verbal sparring, but nothing from Clint."

"Leaving only this message: Don't fuck up! I will personally cut off your balls—including yours, Lynn and Sandy—and grind them into pixie dust. Got it?"

With that, Pat Kovachik turned and sat down. And smiled. Inwardly.

SEVEN

Cutter wasn't really sure how it happened. They never officially lived together. He just sort of started spending nights at her apartment. Sometimes she was at his. A lot of it had to do with finishing work and ending up there. One night, she asked him to come over for Chinese carryout. When it came time for him to go home, she started crying.

"What's wrong?" he asked.

"My back hurts."

He rubbed her lower back until she fell asleep. Forty minutes more, mostly because he did not realize she was asleep. Might have been even longer, but he fell asleep as well. Woke up next to her—she was making snorting sounds—and it was 6:30 in the morning. He watched her sleep for a couple of minutes. He nudged her and she lifted one eyelid.

"You know the thing where I say 'You want to have breakfast?' and you say 'Yeah' and I say 'So should I call you or nudge you?' and you say 'Nudge'?"

"Uh-huh."

"I just nudged you. What's for breakfast?"

"Whatever you make us, big boy," the sleep still in her voice.

He opted for sausage biscuits at the drive thru. As consolation he promised her he would make her a good breakfast. Really. If she would come over tonight, they would get Friday night pizza (pretty much all Davenport pizza sucked so it would have to be from Mac's) and he would fix her breakfast in the morning. She could have the bed. He'd take the couch.

He made a fruit bowl, drop biscuits—really easy, but he was proud of them—and eggs poached in tomato soup. She thought it sounded very weird but had to agree they tasted great.

"Not bad, Chef Boy-Ar-Dee. Now what?"

"Want to run up to the Wapsi?" The Wapsi was in fact the Wapsipinicon River, although no one ever called it anything but the Wapsi. "We can rent a canoe and paddle downstream. It's really nice out."

"Then you should keep it out. Sure. Why not?" Though she would have much preferred that he had suggested they go over to Iowa City to walk around and maybe shop.

They got out an extra set of clothes each. Cutter had canoed enough to know chances were about eighty-twenty they'd end up wet. They jumped into his beat up Camry and made the short drive up. Ninety minutes after breakfast, they were floating down the Wapsi. He did the paddling because after five minutes of her splashing and paddling on the wrong side, he told her he would do it by himself. He strongly suspected her show of ineptitude was not accidental.

He was right, she thought. It really is nice out.

"Why aren't you keeping it?" he asked.

"What?"

"The baby. Why are you going to give it up for adoption?"

She stared at him. Her eyes welled up. She was silent.

"Ah, shit," he thought, "I've fucked up again. I've got to learn when to take a sip."

Finally she answered. "Cutter, I don't know for sure. Some of it is the classic 'Good Catholic girl gets in trouble, goes away to have the baby, gives it up for adoption, goes back home.' Some of it is knowing how my parents would react. Some of it is thinking I just couldn't raise a child by myself. Most of it is being scared to death." She was quiet again.

He paddled slowly. Maneuvered around several newly fallen logs.

"I think you could do it. If your parents can't be supportive, well, screw them. You have lots of friends who can help. I'd help."

"Thanks. I appreciate that. I really do. But I would be so scared of screwing up this child's life. Fatherless. Branded a bastard. Maybe no grandparents. Or aunts and uncles and cousins. I teach at a parochial school and make very little money. I have no savings. Does that seem fair to a child when adoption will guarantee him or her a better life?"

"Geez, Amanda," Cutter argued, "you don't know that for sure. You're young and smart. Beautiful. Funny. I'm sure you could find a good dad. You'll get a better job. And you'll make a great mom."

"How do know that?" She was getting a little angry. "Would you bet a child's well-being on that? Just so you could be a mother?" No response from Cutter. "Well? Would you?"

Cutter was busy paddling them straight into a log which had gotten jammed into the river bank. Dead center, perfect. Any movement was going to either flip the canoe or send then downstream ass first.

Cutter grinned, "Wow. This river is rife with logs."

"Rife? Rife? What the hell kind of thing is that to say? Rife? For God's sake, Cutter." But Amanda smiled. "You ask me those kinds of questions and then you want to talk about the log rifeness of a river? You are a piece of work, Cutter Williams, a real piece of work." She looked at him and felt a new affection for this guy she would have described as "a crazy asshole."

Cutter worked them loose, headed the wrong way, but managed to right the ship without dumping them. He caught her looking at him with an expression he hadn't seen before. Not like he was a guy—good thing, considering the hard-on she had right now for the male of the species. But still, something different.

She spoke. "You want to get away for a few days? You could take me to Chicago. I love Chicago."

"I could. I suppose you want this to be my treat," he replied.

"Of course. Remember I'm a poor pregnant lady." At almost six months you could tell. Amanda wasn't very big to start with and stayed small, but her belly was beginning to look like a bowling ball stuck under her shirt. "And we could buy me some pregger clothes."

"Can we go to a Cubbies game?" he ventured.

Sigh. "I suppose. If we have to." She actually liked going to Wrigley. Her dad had taken her family there several times. She liked it not so much for the baseball but for the crowd, the beautiful grass, the hot dogs, the peanuts and the singing. She didn't let on, so Cutter could think he'd had a say in it.

On Saturday, two weeks later, they were in the cheap seats in left field, hoping a Cards batter would hit a home run to them so they could throw the ball back onto the field. They had spent all day Friday on Michigan Avenue buying her exactly two tops and a pair of stretch jeans. They'd gotten a room with two double beds at the Palmer House. After shopping and dinner they took a cab up to the Kingston Mines for one set from a pretty good blues singer and returned to the hotel. After they had gone to bed, she got up and got into bed beside him. Cutter was suddenly wide awake.

"Don't get any ideas, Stud. I don't want to be touched. I do however want to be held. Think you can do that?"

"I guess." Which he did. He did have to think about things like pond scum and obese old men and pigeons so his body wouldn't send her any unwel-comed messages.

He sat watching the Cubs lose, again. Tough be-ing a Cubs fan. He would sneak looks at her. She was intently trying to throw peanuts at the Cards left field-er, but they mostly didn't even make it to the ivy. He knew he was confused by this. She wasn't making it any easier. What was with the whole climbing into bed with me thing?

Christ in a hand basket.

He made the mental list:

1. She's pregnant.
2. She is not interested in a man.
3. Even if she were, it wouldn't be me.
4. I really like her.
5. She gives up the baby; there is no chance that I could ever change #3. Every time she looked at me, all she would see was the child she had given away.
6. It's not like I'm seeing anyone.

What the hell, maybe helping her is what I am supposed to do. Still, there is something I am missing here. Or maybe she'll keep the baby. Double Christ in a hand basket.

That night he took her to a small Italian restaurant off the beaten path in Boystown. He liked it because it had a courtyard at the rear with half dozen tables and a tree canopy that was hung with old fashioned Christ-mas lights. Mostly he loved the lasagna.

She wore a dress that made her look very pregnant. That is, it was a regular dress she tried to wear one time too many. Five minutes after they sat down, she was back up on her way to pee. Again. The old man, who actually had an Italian accent (though Cutter suspected it was an act) brought over Cutter's glass of wine and said, "So, thisa youra first?"

"What?"

"Youra wife. She's apregnant, with youra first?"

Cutter was confused.

"Youra wife, she's a very bella, pretty. You'a lucky man."

"That I am, sir, that I am. And, yes, it's the first."

"Oh, you'a gonna be a great daddy. I canna tell. You looka so happy." With that, Amanda returned. The old man smiled and bowed, took her hand and kissed it.

Now Amanda was confused. A little embarrassed. "Uh, thanks." To Cutter, after the old man left, "What was that all about?"

"He thinks you're bella."

"What?"

"Pretty. He was telling me how lucky I am to have such a beautiful wife and a baby on the way."

"Oh."

They were silent for several minutes.

"Cutter, I think..."

He cut her off, "I know. It's okay. Really. Just enjoy this. Don't think about next week or next month or next year. Think about only today. Okay?"

They ate and talked. About how they were glad to

be finished with the Humane Society. About his new job, part-time at an ad agency writing copy, about how much they liked Chicago.

The old man was back at the table, "You driva youra car?" he asked Cutter.

"No. Taking the train," Cutter answered.

"Good." He left and returned thirty seconds later with a glass of limoncello. "Ona the house. Bringa good luck. You childrena have'a great healthy child, okay? *Buona fortuna.*"

"*Grazie,*" Cutter said, grinning. Amanda smiled a weak smile and whispered, "Thank you."

On the el, Cuter stood over her. She had her eyes closed and both hands on her belly. Cutter thought, "I wonder what Dad would say. I don't think they ever told us. Were the rules in order of importance or just random. Is it okay to follow 3 and 4, even if it means you break 1 and 2? Or are 1 and 2 to be obeyed first? I'll have to ask him."

EIGHT

By the time they reached the Gulf Stream, the temperature had climbed into the upper eighties and the sun had become an oven broiler. Captain Jefferson cut the *Debbie Lee*'s engines and they drifted rocking gently on the low swells. He came down to see how everyone was doing and told Jordair to set up both the big and smaller fishing rigs. They had passed several other boats, but only one was flying its sailfish flag indicating they had landed, and released, a marlin. The crew of the *Debbie Lee*, as Clint's party now thought of themselves, cheered and hooted at the other boat's victory. After Jordair explained what the flag meant. The landing of the fish and the acknowledgement of the feat by another boat were enough to warrant a new round of drinks on both boats. Ken even convinced the other boat to trade them a bottle of Captain Morgan's Spiced Rum for one of his bottles of vodka.

As they had agreed earlier, Sandy took the chair on the first strike. She was surprised how much fun it was, feeling the fish pulling on the line, struggling to get free, first running away and then doubling back.

She soon got into the flow of reeling and pulling. The fish wasn't large enough to require her being strapped in, but Jordair had insisted she wear a life jacket. After ten minutes, she was flushed and sweating but she was grinning. A few minutes later, Jordair used a large net to bring in her catch, a small wahoo.

Sandy bounced around, "Is it really big? How much does it weigh? Do we keep it or put it back?"

Jordair told her, "It's really a nice fish and you did a terrific job of landing him. Nice work! It is a bit on the small side for a wahoo, but we can put him on ice if you wish. I'm sure we'll get some bigger ones, so you might want to release this one." He was as tactful as possible.

"Oh, yes. Release it. Please." Sandy was suddenly sympathizing with her prey. Jordair let the fish slide back into the ocean where it slapped the surface with its tail and disappeared.

"That was great, Sandy. You're a natural." Clint was genuinely excited for her. "All right, Cutter, you're next," he continued. Before Cutter could respond one of the lines started screaming as it was pulled out to sea.

"Strike!' yelled Jordair. "Who's next?"

Cutter turned toward the mayor and could see that Clint was really into the moment. Cutter said to him, "Hey, Mayor, you take this one. Ken just fixed me a Cuba Libre and I want to drink it before it gets all diluted."

Clint jumped into the chair, needing no further encouragement. Ken told Cutter, "Hey, I thought you wanted a rum and coke. That's what I fixed you." Ken had smoothly made the transition from master sailor to master angler and now to master bartender. "Tell me how to make one of those Cuba things and I'll drink the rum and coke."

"Nah, Ken, this is fine. I like it." Cutter grinned and turned his attention to Clint who was now strapping himself into the Hemingway chair as Jordair cleared the other lines from the water. He watched Clint intently.

Cutter first laid eyes on Clinton Brandsgard the day he interviewed for the job. Though in truth, the interview was one of those politician's tricks to make Cutter feel important. Sandy had already made the decision to hire him. Whatever Sandy decided was so.

It was a Wednesday afternoon and Cutter had been on the job for about six weeks adjusting to the slow pace of the bureaucracy and trying to separate friend from foe. He had discovered that even long time "sorry, we can't do that" bureaucrats appeared to like the mayor and wanted to help him. As yet, he hadn't identified too many enemies.

Cutter was sitting at his desk, wrestling with a press release about how the administration had handled a neighborhood dispute over lights at a park basketball court. "We want the lights down! They attract the wrong element at night." "You mean African-American kids? Is that what you mean?" "Call a spade a spade." It got ugly after that. Until Clint held a neighborhood meeting and brokered a peaceful solution. Which Sandy had actually done prior to the public meeting Clint held. Now Cutter was writing, or trying to write, a release on the peacemaking prowess of His Honor.

Cutter was startled by a hand grabbing his shoulder as Clint flopped down into the chair next to his desk. "Cutter! Whatcha doin?" Clint was smiling.

Cutter was a little taken aback. He stammered, "Uh, I'm working on this press release about…"

Clint cut him off, "Hell with that. It can wait. Let's go down to Mac's and get a beer. You drink beer, doncha?"

Cutter looked at his watch. 3:15.

Clint plowed on, "Hey. This is… Let's see… This is a board meeting and you were just appointed to the board. Board meetings normally occur at 3:00, but I was tied up. Sorry. Let's go."

Ten minutes later they walked into Mac's. The half dozen, happy hour early birds looked up when the flood of sunlight came through the door. The response was almost unanimous. "Hey, Mr. Mayor!" "Mayor, howzit goin?" "You the man, Clint!" Cutter had to admit to himself he kind of liked the attention he was part of. This was different, this having a boss whom people liked. Whom he liked. They took seats in the middle of the bar and Clint said to the bartender, "Black and tan. Two," and held up two fingers.

"Well, shit," thought Cutter, "no beer decisions. This guy is okay."

When the patrons came over to shake hands, wish

him well or ask a question, the mayor was welcoming and warm. It was odd. Clint had made Cutter feel as if he were the only person in the room who mattered to Clint, but Cutter could see Clint managed to make each person feel the same way. A firm handshake here, a hand on the arm there, a leaning in of the head with an air of confidentiality in a whispered response. Cutter took it all in. Every person walked away happy. The bartender was happy. He was hosting the king who was holding court. A true honor.

As folks drifted back to their beers and shots, Clint focused on Cutter. "So, where'dja get a name like Cutter?"

Cutter told him the story about having to wear the "Cutter" sign.

"Really?" asked Clint.

"No," answered Cutter.

Clint looked at him and laughed, loud enough that everyone turned and looked.

"That's pretty fucking funny," the mayor said through a final chuckle. "Where'dja go to high school?" Cutter told him, and since they were only three years apart, they tried to figure out who they might have known in common. The Quad Cities wasn't all that big. Turned out they had played football against each other one year. Well, their teams had. They were both bench warmers so they probably had just stared at each other across the field.

They talked about the area some, about people they knew in common, about sports, but whenever Cutter tried to talk about government or city hall, Clint steered the conversation in another direction. Finally Clint told him, "You know, Cutter, the one rule I have about board meetings is that we don't discuss business."

"Oh. Okay. I have no problem with that. Can I ask how often you have these board meetings?"

"Geez, I don't know, Cutter. This is my first one."

Now it was Cutter's turn to laugh. He turned to the bartender and shot him the victory sign, the universal bar language for "two more". The bartender looked quickly at Clint who nodded his head. As the black and tans arrived, Clint asked, "Hey, you play golf?"

"I play at it. Love the game. Can't break out of the 90s, though."

"Sounds suspiciously like you are trying to set me up to take my money," Clint replied. "Give me your phone."

Cutter handed over his cell phone. Clint dialed a number from memory. "Dan, this is Clint. Great. Everything okay with you? Great. Say, could you get a foursome on at the Arsenal tomorrow? Wait, just a second." He put his hand over the phone and said to Cutter, "Is the Arsenal Club okay or would you rather play at TPC?" Hell, the Arsenal Golf Club was one of the two most exclusive golf clubs in the area and he had never been there, so he replied, "No, no. The Arsenal is fine. But tomorrow is Thursday and…" Clint cut him off with a hand gesture.

Back into the phone, "Yeah, tomorrow at 1:30 or so. Grab some lunch at the club house at noon. Well, you, me, my friend Cutter and, uh, call Paul. See if he'll join us. Great. See you then."

After the round the next day, Clint and Cutter, who had just won twenty dollars in a best ball skins game (largely due to Clint's game), sat having a post round cocktail with their opponents, Dan Callaham, their host, and Paul Morton, Sandy's husband. They were telling jokes and stories on each other, Cutter mostly listening and being entertained. Finally, there was a lull and Cutter sensed they were expecting him to do some entertaining as well.

He asked them, "You know how you can tell if a woman is having a good orgasm?"

They all smiled—guy jokes. At a woman's expense. "No, how?"

"She says 'Oh yes. Oh yes.' And if it is so good it is almost painful?"

"How?"

"Oh no. Oh no." A chuckle. "And if it is almost heavenly?"

"Okay. How?"

"Oh god. Oh god." More laughter. "And do you know what she says if she's faking the orgasm?"

"What?"

"Oh, Clint. Oh, Clint." In the two seconds that passed before there was any reaction, Cutter had the thought, "Oh. My. God. What the fuck have I done? The mayor is going to fire me." The laughter that followed was comedy-club level. And Clint laughed so hard he had tears in his eyes. Whew. Dodged my own bullet there. Suicide by joke.

Two hours later they stumbled out of the bar with

Paul yelling in a loud falsetto, "Oh, Clint. Oh, Clint," and Clint with his arm around Cutter's shoulder.

Over the next months, the board meetings occurred once a week or so. Sometimes the mayor's secretary would call with the message, "Board meeting in twenty minutes." Sometimes Clint would stop at Cutter's desk and collect him. One night, after a particularly rambunctious community meeting, Clint called one after Cutter was almost home.

They played golf some, went to lunch occasionally, shot the shit over a glass of bourbon in the mayor's office. Talked a lot. Clint began asking Cutter's advice on city matters. He didn't always take the advice, but Cutter felt like he was appreciated. Like he was actually making a difference. He liked this guy. And he loved his job. For the first time.

After Cutter had worked for, and hung out with, the mayor for about two years, Clint suddenly seemed to have less time for him. Sure, they still had board meetings occasionally and lunch once in a while, but Clint was busy. Which was okay with Cutter since he had a new girlfriend and she bitched enough about how much time he spent at work and with the mayor. Cutter also had backed into (or been backed into) representing the administration in the arts community.

The arts folks were still pissed, and would be for a long time, at Mayor Brandsgard and that bitch Sandy Morton who had stolen their easy-money funding source. They found, however, that they still needed things from City Hall on occasion, so they made nice and always invited the mayor or his representative to their functions, especially their fundraisers.

That chore would normally have fallen to Sandy in her official capacity, but she wanted less to do with the arts community than they wanted to do with her. Ergo, Cutter got the privilege of being Clint's representative. Cutter found he liked the assignment. Liked the people for the most part. The art patrons were a little boring, but the artists themselves proved to be downright interesting. They served pretty good food and always had open bars. It didn't hurt that his girl-friend got to go and that she loved those events. Made her feel part of the in-crowd of the city and she could endlessly regale her gal pals with stories of who wore what and who was seen with whom.

Still, Cutter missed his time with Clint—regular old guy time. He was also getting a little jealous of Sandy who seemed to get more and more of the mayor's time and attention. But when other people complained that Sandy had too much power and authority, Cutter was always the first to defend her. Over the next year, the group settled into an easy rhythm and found themselves enjoying their jobs and lives. But with the advent of a new campaign, Cutter sensed a growing restlessness.

He was thinking about that restlessness as he watched Clint straining against whatever was on the other end of the line. Whatever it was, it was bigger than anything else they had hooked. The line screamed in agony as it was ripped off the reel. Even with Clint fighting against it, the line kept rolling out.

Cutter looked over at Jordair who was now wearing a very serious expression. Cutter assumed that meant this was the real deal—they were actually going to catch a large sailfish. Jordair busied himself with clearing the deck of any objects, re-checking Clint's safety harness and getting his gaff ready.

Half an hour later, the fish finally broke the surface. To Cutter, it looked huge. Everyone was now on deck and the sight of the marlin brought sounds of amazement from the entire group. Lynn had moved next to Clint and was rubbing his arms, though Cutter thought the rubbing was more for her than him. Lynn squealed with delight when they saw the fish. Her husband was not only a politically powerful man, he was also a he-man. She even offered to get him a drink. Which she ordered Ken to bring.

Over the next forty-five minutes, Clint worked his ass off. Reeling, tugging, pulling, horsing and fighting the marlin. It was exhausting. Clint could feel the fight going out of the fish. "Almost there, sir," Jordair encouraged. "Keep working him for just a little longer and you'll have yourself a trophy fish."

Ten minutes later, the marlin made one last ditch dive, but Clint kept the line taut and the dive was stopped. The line went slack for a few seconds, then the sea erupted as the marlin leapt completely out of the water, made one fluid twist of its entire body and snapped the line in two. Gone. All that work and now the fish was gone in two seconds. Everyone was silent until Ken said, "Aw, man, that's too bad. That sucks."

The mayor put the rod back in the holder, unbuckled the safety harness and slowly stood up. He stretched, turned toward the group and said, in a very quiet voice, "Wow. That was the most fucking fun I have ever had in my life. Ever. I cannot wait until it is my turn again. Somebody fix me a drink." Relieved laughter all around.

Captain Jefferson had cut the engines and let the *Debbie Lee* drift and joined the group on the deck. "Too bad, Mr. Mayor," he offered. "That was a very nice fish. Sorry we couldn't get it onto the boat for you. You know how it is, though. A lot like winning votes. Sometimes you work and work for that one vote and at the last minute, it gets away."

Clint grinned at the captain, and in a perfect imitation of the Cowardly Lion, said, "Ain't it the truth. Ain't it the truth."

NINE

Cutter's part time gig at the ad agency mostly required him to sit at a desk and try to be clever. It was a small local agency whose primary business came from small local companies. Used car dealers, restaurants, grocery stores and bars. Lots of bars. Judging from the number of ads they did for bars and clubs, one might surmise that the Quad Cities had a drinking problem. One might be correct. Cutter had found there were only so many ways you could say, "Come get your drunk on," in an ad.

So when his boss offered him an opportunity to be part of a proposal team for a new big ad campaign, Cutter jumped at it. Even after his boss explained that unless they got the new account, he couldn't pay Cutter for the work he would put into the proposal and presentation. Ramrod had set up a new subsidiary, the Cerf Company, to market and sell a newly-developed product, a small, alternative fuel tractor. They had decided to market the tractor that way because there was a chance there might be a backlash to the product and they feared that backlash might damage their brand.

Lots of Ramrod customers made their living by growing corn. Corn which was used to make ethanol which was used as a supplement in gasoline. Corn, which the U.S. Government heavily subsidized for just that use. A product that didn't use gasoline might not be welcomed in that part of the country.

Cutter's firm was one of three local agencies that would compete for the work. Apparently it had been strongly suggested to Cerf executives to use a local business. Suggested by Gerald Huntsman. Which made it, of course, a fine suggestion. Cutter enjoyed the give and take of the creative team and within a few days they had devised their strategy and worked through the presentation details. Cutter even agreed to get a haircut and not wear jeans to be part of the presentation.

Cutter's team filed into the conference room and set up their boards and materials. Within minutes the Cerf team arrived and, after greetings were exchanged by the team leaders, they all sat down across from each other, Cutter at the far end of the table. Low man on the totem pole. To be seen and not heard. Unless of course they got desperate. He was seated two down from a very lovely young blond woman, Cerf's legal eagle, who looked oddly familiar to Cutter. He surreptitiously stared at her.

Twenty minutes later they took a break. The blonde immediately came over to Cutter and put out her hand, "You're Cutter Williams, aren't you?" Cutter could only bob his head in answer. "It's me, Cutter.

Karen Stuart. From Northwestern. English comp."
Well, Christ in a hand basket. He remembered Karen
Stuart, but this was not the way she looked. Definitely
not. Karen had been dumpy. Hawk nose. Mousy hair.
Smart and funny, but arf. And this girl was decidedly
not arf.

"Karen, I would never have recognized you.
You've, uh, er, changed so much. You look great."
Now Cutter couldn't shut up. "What are you doing
here? Last I heard you were in law school back East.
How? What?" he stammered.

"Yep. Got a law degree, worked for a firm back in
Chicago for a year and then got offered this job. I'd
never been to the Quad Cities before but I like it. How
did you get here?"

"I grew up here and came back home after college." They were interrupted by the meeting being
called back in session. Every time he looked at her, he
saw her smiling at him. When the meeting broke up,
Cutter's team was assured they would hear promptly
about the selection, and the Cerf executives quickly left
the room. On her way out, Karen walked by Cutter
and handed him a slip of paper and said, "Call me. I
would love to see you again." The piece of paper had
all three of her phone numbers on it.

Imagine that. True ugly duckling story.

They didn't get the account. Waste of a fucking
haircut.

Cutter was sitting at Amanda's kitchen table and
having his second cup of coffee, trying to pick the lint

from his brain. He was thinking about the time he had wasted on the stupid Cerf proposal which led him to thinking about Karen. Maybe he should call her. This Amanda thing sure didn't seem to be going anywhere. With that thought, he heard her flush the toilet. For the fourth time in the last six hours.

She waddled into the kitchen, rubbed his head as she passed and put the kettle on to make some tea. She sat down next to him and gave him a warm, but syrupy-eyed look.

"Morning." Her voice still had some sleep in it.

"Mornin', sunshine. How you feelin'?" he asked.

"Okay. Hey, Cutter, I have a favor to ask."

"Sure. What is it?"

"I can't see you for a couple of days, like Thursday through Sunday. Would that be alright?" Her voice was tenuous.

"I guess." He didn't like this. Wasn't sure why, but it didn't sound good.

"Terry is coming through town and I told him he could stay here. I hope that's okay," she told him.

"Hey, it's your apartment and your life." Downright pissy.

"Don't be that way."

"Amanda, you should do what you want. Does Terry know about that?" He pointed at her stomach. "You probably shouldn't let that be a surprise."

"Yes. I told him. You know, this is just a visit. Nothing more. He and I are over. He knows it; I know it. Old friends."

"Yeah, sure. I'll grab my stuff and take it with me this morning. Give you a couple of days to get ready."

"Cutter, please…"

The next day, she called him two times and he let it go to voice mail. She called again on Friday and then Saturday morning. All to voice mail. She left no messages.

Cutter knew it was for exactly the wrong reason but it didn't stop him. He called Karen and invited her for drinks and dinner on Friday. Took her to the Faithful Pilot, out of spite, since he now thought of the Pilot as his and Amanda's place. He was sure that Amanda never even thought of the place.

Cutter and Karen had a nice enough evening, catching up on post college days, reminiscing about Northwestern and Chicago, sharing their current employment stories. She apologized for his team's not being selected. She had wanted Cutter to do the work, but her vote didn't count for much. He really wanted to ask about the change in her appearance, but decided that was too tacky, even for him.

After dinner, he drove the back way into Davenport to "show her some of the area she may not have seen." Which, entirely coincidentally, took them right by Amanda's apartment in the Heights. Where Cutter slowed and saw movement in the brightly lit window. Made him feel like shit. For two reasons. He was spying. And they were in there. Christ in a hand basket. What the fuck was wrong with him.

"Cutter, are you okay?" Karen asked as he

dropped her off. "I remember you being pretty, I don't know, 'up' all the time. You seem distracted. I hope it's not me."

"No. No. Sorry. You know, sometimes life just gets in the way of living."

"Hey," she asked, "I know this is last minute, but tomorrow night I have this reception I have to go to for work. You wanna go with? My treat."

"Yeah. Sure. That would be great. Thanks. And I promise to be better company," he told her.

And he was.

Terry and Amanda started dating in college. They sure didn't look like they fit together. She was petite and reserved; he was burly, with long red hair and a full red beard, and loud. She was a "nice girl;" he was a "bad boy." He rode a motorcycle; she drove a Volvo. She was a virgin, he was very experienced. It didn't take him long to bed her. She was in love. He told her he was.

Over the next three years they had an on-again, off-again relationship. He would piss her off and she would become a screaming meanie until he had enough and left. Within days she would be asking him to come back and then she couldn't keep her hands off of him. He was always happy to be back in bed with her. Not that he was an asshole. That was just what her friends claimed. What did they know?

A couple of hours before Terry was due to arrive (and five hours before he actually did, without calling), Amanda found herself getting ready for his arrival like

85

she did in the early days of their relationship. Long bath, hair done, best outfit and makeup. She looked in the mirror. Wow, I look pretty good. Then she noticed her belly and started to cry. Had to do the makeup thing all over again.

She couldn't believe how excited she was to see him. Pacing the floor nervous. Pee every fifteen minutes nervous. Think I'm gonna puke nervous. He was just like she remembered. Only better. He had shaved his beard and cut his hair. Looked like he had been spending some time in the gym. She got that warm feeling that started in her chest and wound its way down to her, well, all the way down. She caught herself. No. No. No. Gave him a non-committal hug.

They talked for a few hours and got caught up on what they had been doing for the last year. About his job and her job. About his family and her family. Not once did he ask about the pregnancy or about the father or about the baby or what she was going to do. So she avoided the subject as well. She fixed him dinner and they ate. Afterwards, they sat on the couch and listened to the music they used to share. He drank wine and she drank stale ginger ale. She wanted some pictures of him, so she got her camera and they took turns shooting photos of each other, along with a couple of two person self-portraits.

She was getting tired, what with her nerves being on edge all day and then the excitement and her not-to-be-discussed condition. She leaned forward to stretch her back and Terry reached over and started to rub her neck. It felt so good. She just kind of melted and moved in toward him to urge him to keep rubbing. He rubbed her neck and then her shoulders, massaging the tension right out of them. He moved his hands down her back, massaging as he went. It still felt good. He got down to the really sore part of her lower back and suddenly she saw Cutter's face and felt his hands rubbing that ache out, like he had done so many times. She sat bolt upright, surprising herself almost as much as she surprised Terry.

"What?" he asked.

"I need to go to bed," she said. "Right now."

"You bet. Let's go to bed." He was all for that.

"I'm sorry. I mean I have to go to bed. You are sleeping here on the couch. I'll talk with you in the morning. Good night." She got up and walked into her bedroom and closed the door. He thought he heard it lock.

The next morning Amanda got up, dressed in her stretch jeans and a sweatshirt, tucked her hair into a ball cap, and marched out of her bedroom.

"Good morning," she told Terry. "Would you like some scrambled eggs for breakfast?"

"That'd be fine. Coffee?" he wondered.

"In a minute. But we need to talk." Ah, shit. "I know I said you could stay here while you're in town, but you can't. You have to leave this morning. I'm sorry," she said. And she was. But she really didn't want him around anymore. She wasn't sure why. She'd have to think about it. But she was certain of it. He was

87

gone thirty minutes later. Out of her life. Forever, as it turned out.

Cutter wouldn't answer her calls, and she figured he had a right to be upset. What had she been thinking? She hadn't, that was it. Terry had never given her anything but grief and heartache. Okay, there was the great sex and they did have fun together, but he hadn't even asked about the baby. Hadn't once offered any help. Hell, not even any consolation. Cutter. Sweet, dear Cutter. He had come along at the wrong time. Wrong for him, perfect for her. All right, I'll beg for forgiveness. If he'll just take my fucking calls. Prick.

Monday morning Cutter called her from work. She was curt. He was curt. How are you? Fine. You? Fine. Want to have dinner? I guess. What time? Seven. Chinese? Okay. Bye. Bye.

He picked her up five minutes early (good sign?) and they drove, in silence, to the restaurant.

How was your day? Fine. Yours? Fine. Did you have a good week? Okay. How was your visit with Terry? Short. What? I asked him to leave after twelve hours.

It broke the ice. He felt better. She felt better. He ordered an airplane gin and tonic. The waitress wanted to know what that was and he explained, "You know, when you get a gin and tonic on an airplane, they give you a three ounce plastic cup filled with ice and a one and a half ounce bottle of gin, which leaves room for about one half ounce of tonic." The waitress laughed and brought him exactly what he wanted. Amanda's doctor had given her the all clear for "NO MORE than two glasses of wine per week," so she ordered a red wine, wondering if that would go with General Tso's Chicken, deciding that red wine went with everything.

They talked. He told her about running into an old college chum and going out with her. Amanda surprised herself with her reaction—she feigned pleasant interest, but found that she had bitten the inside of her lip enough to draw blood. Bitch. Harlot. Slut. She devoured her food and asked if they could go to Whitey's for ice cream after. They did. She asked him if he could spend the night.

"I have to work in the morning and I didn't bring my stuff," he responded.

"Please."

He couldn't say "no" to that face.

They were at her apartment, she was busy in the bathroom, getting ready for bed and he yelled, "Okay if I use your computer to check my email?"

"Sure. Just no porn sites," she half kidded.

When he logged on, he noticed that new pictures had been downloaded, so he checked to make sure she was not watching and he looked through them. Some were of a good looking guy he assumed, correctly, must be Terry. Some of her Terry had apparently taken. A couple of the two of them together.

After making sure that Amanda was safely ensconced in the bathroom (her getting-ready-for-bed routine still managed to consume thirty minutes, plus one or two pees), he looked at the pictures of Terry. It didn't make him less jealous. Everything he knew about Terry was what Amanda had told him. No personal experience. No one else to talk to who knew him. So like anybody else, Cutter let his imagination fill in the blanks. He created a whole person out of a few photographs and the few things that Amanda had told him. What he was like, what he did and said, how he acted, how he treated Amanda. Was it an accurate picture? Didn't matter. It was Cutter's whole truth.

He studied a picture of Amanda. She had an expression he had not seen. Her head was turned slightly downward. Her eyes were a little closed, but were shiny. Warm. There was a slight glow to her cheeks. The corners of her mouth turned up, ever so slightly. Relaxed and warm. A look he had not seen. But a look he could figure out. Cutter let his imagination fill in the blanks, again. She was besot. She was in love. It crushed him.

TEN

The excitement of the lost marlin died down and everyone in the group was feeling the effects of the fishing, the alcohol, the heat and the sun. They had all made their way to places to lie down. Cutter, Pat and Lynn in their quarters, Ken in the hammock on the rear deck and Sandy and Clint on towels on the front sunning deck. Only Clint was awake, still feeling the effects of the adrenaline from his epic battle. Young man and the sea. He had tried to relive the battle with Sandy but she seemed irritable and not the least bit interested. Five minutes later she was asleep. But, damn, it just couldn't get any better, could it?

Captain Jefferson had asked them if they were going to want to do any night fishing. Ken asked what they would catch at night. "Shark," answered the captain. Being that his profession made him feel a strong kinship to sharks, Ken was all for it. As was Clint. He wanted another shot at a big fish. The rest of them rebelled. They wanted to relax, have a nice dinner. Samantha had promised them hors d'oeuvres with cocktails, followed by steaks and baked potatoes with copious amounts of wine. Chocolate sundaes for dessert.

Captain Jefferson headed the *Debbie Lee* northeast, planning to let it drift back southwest with the current during the night. Bad enough having to split the night watch between just him and Jordair, he didn't want to have to be piloting and navigating at the same time. At least this group was an amicable bunch. Not like the last party, which he had had to take back to shore in the middle of the night. The seven former Ohio State frat brothers had gotten all drunked up and made passes at Samantha and Jessica, who quit the moment her feet touched dry land. And Jessica had been trained enough to be able to take a night watch, unlike Samantha. Tom thought Clint's outing would probably make it through the night. But he and Jordair would be tired.

By six o'clock, Jordair had cleaned and stowed all the rigs, re-iced the bait well and secured the rest of the boat. He was getting a few hours of sleep before his four hour watch began at ten o'clock. Samantha was preparing the hors d'oeuvres: cold shrimp, small crab cakes and her own recipe for a spicy guacamole. Sandy, who had showered and changed back into shorts and a light sweater after her nap, was keeping Samantha company. Samantha had arranged all the food on platters and was mixing a pitcher of frozen margaritas in a blender.

"You want a margarita? They're very good, if I do say so myself," Samantha offered.

"No. No thank you. But could I try the guacamole? It looks wonderful," Sandy answered.

As soon as she took a large bite of the guacamole, Sandy's eyes lit up. "Hot!" she said as she fanned her mouth.

"Yeah. Good, isn't it?" Samantha said. "Now you want that margarita?"

"No, but some lemonade would be great."

Samantha finished arranging food and drinks and napkins and glasses. Sandy helped her take things up on deck. The air was cooling quickly, though it was still warm. Everyone except Ken was on deck, reading or watching the ocean. Pat was on his laptop. As soon as the women showed up with food, Cutter went below and rousted Ken, who was beet red and whining about the sunburn pain. Two of Samantha's icy drinks made it all better. Ken lavished the praise on her. Still, he seemed to be making no headway. Looked like there would be no romance on the high seas tonight.

They had a wonderful dinner. They all agreed that it was perfect. Though Lynn had asked Samantha if she "could cook this steak just a tiny bit more." As they finished the sundaes, Clint reminded them there was still some work to do and asked them to meet on deck in thirty minutes. More drinks optional. Since romance was not in the air, Ken knew he would take the option. Samantha asked if there was anything she could get them for their meeting, was told "No. But thank you," and she started cleaning up.

Forty-five minutes later, they were all assembled.

Mayoral face back on, Clint told them, "Okay, Sandy, you're on. Share this new initiative which we are all going to ride into the statehouse." He sat down and Sandy took his place.

"I'm excited. I hope you all like this idea. I think it is important to us and to the community. And that you will all help me, us, work through the details. We're probably going to need some outside help as well, and maybe you can identify where that help can come from."

"Come on, Sandy, get on with it." Patience was not Lynn's strong suit.

Sandy continued, "What are the three things every parent wants for their children? To be happy. To be healthy. And to have a chance to make a good life. We can't do much to guarantee the first. We've gone a long way with the tuition program toward helping with the chance for a good life. What most people don't know is the tuition program, largely due to the great tuition deals the State schools are giving us and matching money that is coming in, is currently running a large surplus. We are going to recommend the surplus be used to tackle the children's health issue."

"First, all children in Davenport under the age of eighteen will be guaranteed first-class health care, available to their parents on a sliding scale, costs being low enough in all cases as to not put a burden on the family's finances. Not routine health department/free clinic care, but all children will have a regular doctor who would be their physician until they reach eighteen.

In-depth physicals every year. Proactive, individualized health plans. But we don't think that medical care is enough. We want our program to stress healthy life styles. Develop healthy habits in kids."

"The schools will re-introduce physical education and make it a part of every day's classes for every grade level. We will work with the Y and other community organizations to get every child enrolled in some kind of physical activity, paying class costs for those who can't afford it. Our own parks department will offer summer camps which stress physical well-being. We want to get kids off their butts and away from television and computers and out into the fresh air. Bike paths. Soccer fields. More spaces that encourage community play."

"The schools will also devote more resources to healthy food. Not just what they serve for lunch, but also to teaching every kid about how to choose food, how to fix food and what all you need to eat to stay feeling good. This won't be only for kids who take Home Ec—do they even teach that anymore?—but for every student. We also want to explore the idea of taxing, and I mean taxing the shit out of, junk food, whether it is from the grocery or the fast food place, that money going to supplement and thus lower the cost of healthy food. Make healthy food cheaper than junk food."

"These two programs will make Davenport THE place to raise your family. If we also continue to manage growth and prevent urban sprawl, we are well on our way to building the best city in the U.S."

Sandy stopped to catch her breath. They had all seen her fired up before, but this was a new level. Clint beamed. Pat smiled a genuine smile. Only Lynn appeared uninterested. Until Clint reminded her this program would take them into the statehouse. And maybe further. If they would all work together and pull it off. The business community and the health care community would be behind it. Mr. Huntsman was going to make sure that happened.

Clint continued, "Pat, explain how this figures into the campaign."

Pat stood. "The week after the other party decides who their sacrificial lamb is going to be, Clint will hold a press conference—Cutter, it will be important to get the Des Moines press in for this somehow—along with the Superintendent of the schools and the CEO of the health care system in Davenport. They will announce their plan to jointly approach the State legislature about widening the use of the gambling dollars for this program. The Superintendent will also announce the formation of a committee to work on the Phys Ed and food issues. Then we wait for the other candidate's reaction."

Based on the questions and comments from the group, Sandy felt as if she had another winning initiative. Something to make a difference in people's lives. Something important. Something Clint would appreciate and that would make her indispensable to him. They spent another hour or so on the topic, mostly Cutter making notes and working out the PR angle of it. Ken spent time trying to shoot holes in it, happy when he couldn't.

They broke up, Pat back to his laptop, Lynn back to her stateroom, Ken back to a glass of bourbon and his pursuit of Samantha, Cutter to the table with his note pad, already itching to write about this. Clint looked at Sandy, once again with wonder in his eyes. "Let's get a drink and go up on deck," he said, moving to the bar. "What would you like?" as he poured bourbon over ice for himself.

"Soda water with a lime," she answered. He poured it and then handed her the drink and they went topside toward the bow of the *Debbie Lee*. With only a sliver of a moon and no other boat lights in sight, the stars were almost overwhelming. It had cooled into the seventies and there was only the hint of a sea breeze. The Mary Poppins of evenings. Practically perfect in every way.

"Clint, I'm pregnant."

He stared at her, no response at all. Finally, a huge, forced grin and then, "Gee, that's terrific. I didn't know you and Paul were trying to have a kid. When is it due?" Trying to figure out if it would disrupt the campaign somehow.

"No, Clint," starting to get angry. "It's not Paul's. It's yours." Tears in her eyes.

"It can't be. We always used protection. Don't be telling me this. I love you, but we can't have a baby. Not now. You know we have to get to the governor's office before we can divorce Lynn and Paul and get married." His turn to get angry. "It must be Paul's."

Very quietly, she responded, "No, Clint, listen. This baby we are going to have is yours. Paul is infertile. He can't make a baby. With me or with anyone else. I have already seen an attorney to start the divorce action. You need to talk to Ken or whomever to start yours. I can hide this pregnancy and we can hide the relationship until after the election, but I want to be married before our child is born."

"We can't do that, Sandy. Listen to reason. The time is just not right. You have to get an abortion."

The affair was bound to happen. Clint Brandsgard was taken with her from the minute she railed on about the public money going into the arts. She was beautiful and smart. Could handle herself with all kinds of people. She was passionate. Her husband was a lout. A necessary lout, but still a lout. He had looked for ways to spend more time with her from the beginning, including her in meetings, telling her they would have to do some important (to her) piece of work over lunch or dinner.

The more time he spent with her, the more he was attracted to her. But it was more. He found he really did like her as well. Started to rely on her abilities to help him do his job. She made him a much better mayor. Confided in her. Made an effort to be a real friend to her. Not like the bank lady. The bank lady was great looking and even better in bed, but that was pretty much the beginning and end of her assets.

When she first went to work for him, Sandy was so excited to be a part of something and to make a difference. It was overwhelming. This man she worked for, this very attractive and personable man, treated her with a respect and esteem she had never encountered before. Second fiddle to her brothers when she was growing up, even though she was the star student, wooed and then pretty much ignored and treated as chattel by Paul, unable to have a baby, no job because Paul wanted a stay-at-home wife. Clint made her laugh. He had given her life meaning. No, better than that, he had given her a chance for her to give her own life meaning.

She didn't want to, but the attraction and kindness, the nearness and the appreciation, it all made her fall in love with him. She wouldn't tell him. Hell, she wouldn't even admit it to herself. But she knew it was there. She found she had to be careful when she was around him not to stare at him. Other people would be able to see.

Eventually, in the course of a late dinner, he told her how he felt. She didn't want to react, but she was so happy she almost screamed. Knew she shouldn't be, but, still. When he took her back to her car at City Hall, he looked around and then hugged her. She didn't want to, but she hugged him back. From that point on, one touch led to another, one intimate moment to another, to kissing, to touching her. She was able to stop it at that, and, to her surprise, he didn't push her. She knew how much he wanted her, but he appeared to want her friendship more.

Paul was being even more of an asshole than

normal. Bitching about her working so much. Bitching about her boss. Spending lots of time with his drinking buddies. Which sometimes included her boss. At least, she told herself, he was being more of an asshole. She needed him to be an asshole. For her own peace of mind. Sometimes if you try hard enough, a person will give you the shit you want from them. Even Lynn had become more of a self-serving bitch. Thoughtful of her.

Clint asked Sandy if she wanted to go to a Livable Cities Conference in Charleston, South Carolina. By now she had made up her mind to go to bed with him. She knew that it was always the woman who made the decision for that step. What was it they said? A woman needs a reason to sleep with someone. A man needs an opportunity. In Charleston, they would both have what they needed. She bought new underwear.

The sex was better than either one expected. He was considerate and did things to her that no one else ever had. Which made her do things she had never done. The physical relationship did not negatively affect the rest of the relationship. Fact was, it made it better. Sure, they had to sneak around, lie and cover up. But there was a mutual trust neither had experienced before. It wasn't long until they started talking about the future. Getting to the statehouse, marrying each other, having children and his plan to run for President.

Married and having children when the time was right. What was she thinking? Was she thinking? Everything we have worked for, gone. How could she do this to him? She should see what the answer is. He shouldn't even have to be the one to bring it up. If she really loved him and understood and believed in him, he would never have known. She would have dealt with it. It's not that big a deal nowadays. It would be much better for her as well.

"No, Clint. No. I am not going to have an abortion. I can't even fucking believe you would suggest that. I know this isn't a good time, but you won't have any trouble getting reelected. In two years, we will be the happy couple with a small child and no one, certainly no one on the state level, will remember anything else. I can understand why you are upset, but you need to think this through. You know you can trust me. We can make this work. We will make this work." She reached out to hold him and felt him shrink from her, though just for a second. He hugged her back.

"How far along are you?"

"Five weeks." He did the math in his head, both backwards and forwards. Yeah, it could be his. Probably was. She could hide it until after the election. Tell people she was getting fat. Even her getting a divorce wouldn't upset the apple cart, unless Mr. Huntsman got pissed about her divorcing his guy. But Huntsman didn't seem like the kind of person who would let a little thing like having an unhappy minion keep him from getting his way. There was no way, though, he could divorce Lynn before then. Or even let her know something was wrong. Sandy would just have to live with that.

He would have to tell the others. Ken absolutely needed to know. Make sure he was legally protected from any fallout. Pat, of course. Cutter, he supposed, because he was smart enough to figure it out any way. Maybe they could figure a way to get him, them, through this.

"Okay, Babe. Don't worry. We'll figure it all out. I love you," he told her.

"I'm sorry, Clint. I didn't mean for this to happen. But I'm happy it did. Bad timing, but it's what we wanted. I love you, too."

Dammit to hell. This is gonna get worse before it gets better. Huntsman will be pissed. He warned me about my little soldier. Fuck. He threw his glass overboard.

ELEVEN

In June, Cutter's firm caught a huge break and signed a contract for an ad campaign which included print, electronic media and the internet. The campaign was to be intense, but short lived. It was all hands on deck. Cutter went from twenty-five hours a week to three straight weeks of sixty hours plus. Because they delivered on time and under budget, the firm earned a bonus, which the owner, in an unusual fit of generosity, divided among the staff. Cutter had earned enough extra to cover his own budget for another whole month, plus the bonus. He decided to reward himself, and Amanda, with a vacation. Plus replace his treadless tires.

Amanda was excited. She called her doctor and got the okay to travel at least for three more weeks. Cutter allowed her to choose where, as long as his three conditions were met: 1. had to stay in budget; 2. had to be salt water there; and 3. had to have golf courses. Over the next couple of days, as Cutter finished up a few things at work, she scoured the internet. Decided, because it was off season, they would go to Fort Myers Beach. Florida sunshine. Off season fares and prices. They could stay right on the beach. Three days later, on Sunday, they landed in the ninety-two degree sunshine. An hour after that, they had checked into the hotel and were having boat drinks under the tiki hut. Hers was virgin; his was not.

The following morning, they walked down to Times Square and had breakfast at a Greek restaurant. Odd choice for a beach restaurant. Turned out the fare was pretty standard southern breakfast: something fried, grits, pig parts and a Coke. With hot sauce on the side. Afterwards they walked up the beach to Bowditch Park—he threw stones into the water, she tried to collect shells, but found her belly got in the way and gave up the effort. She held his hand as they walked back down the beach. They spent the rest of the day on the beach, sunning, reading and sleeping in the sun.

On Tuesday he played golf. He'd checked into local courses and found that twenty minutes away was the Fort Myers Country Club, the oldest course in that part of the country, designed by Donald Ross. Terrific. Classic Florida golf. When he got to the course, he was disappointed. It was totally flat and looked to be no challenge at all. Nice clubhouse. Cathy took his money and paired him up with a couple of locals. The pro asked her why she would put him with those two guys, and she laughed. Must be an inside joke.

Turned out the two guys were old codgers— actually, probably only in their sixties, but old to him. They looked like Mutt and Jeff with shaggy white moustaches. They ended up being entertaining to play alongside. They had a running shtick which consisted of giving each other shit about everything, from golf swings to clothing choices to wives. And especially about the dollar-a-hole bet they had, which pretty much seemed to be their entire *raison d'etre*. The course turned out to be substantially more difficult than it looked. Hole seventeen took three of his new golf balls and ten strokes. He joined Mutt and Jeff for a beer on the veranda of the clubhouse after the round. There they argued over liars' poker.

Cutter watched an even older couple finish the eighteenth hole. When the old man made a long putt, the woman clapped and rushed over to give him a kiss. He followed their slow progress as they came onto the veranda and ordered drinks. Thought about how nice it would be to have that when you were old. He wasn't sure why, but watching them he was hit by an over-powering urge—he had to ask Amanda to marry him. Keep the baby. Have a family. Maybe she wasn't in love with him. But he knew she liked him. They were good together.

At dinner, Amanda announced, "I want to play golf with you tomorrow." Cutter laughed.

"I don't think in this heat and in your condition you would enjoy learning golf very much."

"No, not real golf. Putt-putt. Please, can we play putt-putt?"

After breakfast, they drove to the nearest minia-ture golf course and played. Two rounds. She was terrible. She squealed with delight every time the ball went in the hole. The layout featured a dozen very large fiberglass animals, including a ten foot tall rooster. She loved the story he always told about his pet chicken and made him pose beside it so she could take his picture.

They drove out to Sanibel for seafood at the Lazy Flamingo. After they ordered, she said to him, "You know, you've told me about your pet chicken and stupid stories about how you got your name, but you really haven't told me much about your real life."

"What do you want to know?" he answered.

"I don't know. Girlfriends. What you were really like in high school. About college. You know, your history. What makes Cutter, Cutter."

"Well, it all started in a log cabin in the mountains of Kentucky," he began.

"No. C'mon, Cutter," she was not smiling. "Real stuff. Have you ever had a serious girlfriend?"

"Sort of. I guess. Not anything I really like to talk about."

"In high school?" Her interest was suddenly piqued.

"No, not in high school. I went to an all-boys' Catholic school. Our love life, least for most of us, consisted of a couple of dances with the girls' school and looking at dirty pictures on the net."

"You really want to know?" he went on.

"I do."

"It's embarrassing. I was young and stupid."

She smiled. "Well, at least you're not so young anymore."

"My freshman year at Northwestern, I was taking an English Lit class and we were reading Conrad's *Heart of Darkness*."

"Great book," Amanda interrupted.

"You've read it?" he asked, sounding a lot more incredulous than he meant to.

"Yes. You're not the only one who can read, Smart ass."

He was embarrassed. "So you want me to tell you or not?"

"Oh, please do," she said, a little smugly.

He picked up his story, "The professor asked us about Conrad's description of the essence of truth. Whether or not it rang true. I had actually been amazed by it, so my hand shot up and I was all over lauding Conrad for his insight. You know, at eighteen, I knew pretty much everything there was to know about truth." Amanda laughed and he went on, "Anyway, this guy in the back of the room yells 'Bullshit' and goes on to say he thought O'Brien was much closer in his description in *The Things They Carried* because, like him, O'Brien had actually been in a war. What could I say? I had nothing. I shrank down in my chair and took a sip out of the shut-the-fuck-up cup."

"After class I was on my way to Norris, the student union, and Chuck—that was the ex-soldier's name—catches up to me and asks if I want to get a cup of coffee. I say 'sure' and we go to Norris. We get coffee and sit down and he reaches in his backpack and hands me a copy of the O'Brien book. Says, 'Here, read this. You'll like it.' We talk. Long enough that we are still talking when it is time to switch from coffee to beer. I like the guy. He is smart and funny and has had an entirely different life from me."

"Oh my God, Cutter! Don't tell me your first love was with a gay guy?"

Cutter laughed, "Oh, no. Most certainly not. But thanks for the thought. Maybe that's how you see me."

"Not at all." She was serious.

"Anyway, we started hanging out together. He was about four years older, married and lived off campus. His wife was a nurse who worked the night shift at a hospital, so lots of nights we hung out at his place. He was soon the best friend I had ever had. I got to know his wife as well. Her name was Tommie. She didn't look like any Tommie I had ever seen before. I liked her. A lot."

Amanda shook her head. "And you got a crush on her. I've heard about dating the roomie's sister, but, geez, Cutter."

"It gets worse. Lots worse. You sure you want to hear this?" She nodded. "Toward the end of the year... I can't believe I'm telling you this. I've never told anyone. Toward the end of the year, I spent the night on their couch. Chuck had early classes, told me to hang around 'til he got back. That Tommie would be home from work soon. I went back to sleep. The next thing I know, Tommie is lying down next to me. I like it, but I don't like it as well. She tells me that she has fallen in love with me. Wants us to go upstairs to the bedroom. I want to, but I can't do it, on account of Chuck."

"What happened then?" Amanda wanted to know.

"We spent weeks exchanging looks and secretive touches and finally end up in bed together. After I convince myself Chuck doesn't appreciate her. Or some such shit. I felt terrible, but I was in love. With my best friend's wife."

"Winston Weller Williams, why do you tell me these big stories? I was being serious," she complained.

Now he was serious. "Actually, this is true. I was in love. Crazy. Every chance I got I would go see her. After two months, I waited for her at the hospital and begged her, "You have to leave Chuck. I'll leave school and get a job and we can get married. She took my hand—I will never forget this—and told me, 'Oh, Cutter, no. This was just a fun thing. We can't get married. I'm sorry. I would never leave Chuck. And you're just a boy.' I was crushed. Embarrassed. Humiliated. Hurt."

"I decided, then and there, never to share how I felt with a girl. They couldn't be trusted. If I ever felt that way again. I kept that promise. At least, I have 'til now."

She let the last comment slide. "What happened to Chuck?"

"I felt so bad. This guy had been a good friend and I betrayed him. Over a woman. I think I pushed him away, at least subconsciously. Punished myself for being such a shit." She reached across the table, took his hand and gave it a little squeeze. Let it go. She was a little surprised. She realized she had never seen any pain in his eyes before, but there was some now. She felt a little sorry for him.

"So how did you really get your name?"

The smile came back into his eyes. Familiar territory. Much better. "I hated my name. Win was okay. Some of my buddies called me that and it was pretty cool. But most kids called me Winnie or Winnie the Pooh. Then in middle school this asshole teacher said, 'Winston. Oh. As in Winston Churchill.' Then he made a bulldog face, used a British accent and quipped, 'My name is Winston and this, this is our finest hour.' The other kids thought it was hilarious and for the next year, someone would say it to me at least once a day. The only good thing to come out of it was a few years later when the high school drama club put on *The Importance of Being Earnest*, every kid in high school could do a pretty fair English accent. I had had enough. I decided I wanted a really cool nickname. Something with panache. Élan. Of course, I didn't know those words, but I happened to watch an old movie, *M*A*S*H*, and these really cool surgeons in the movie referred to each other as Cutter. I adopted it. Refused to answer to anything else. Even in class. By the time I was a senior, it finally worked."

She had to ask, "Is that the true story?"

He held his up hand, palm forward, three middle fingers pointing up and the thumb and little finger touching in front of the palm, "Scout's honor."

Over the next couple of days, Cutter played golf two more times. On Thursday, Amanda stayed at the beach. But on Friday, she went with him and drove the cart. Halfway through the round, she started whining about how boring golf was, and wondering why anyone would waste time doing it. She did, however, love seeing the alligators roaming the course. Not so much the big green snake. She did have to agree how lovely the course was. He did not play very well. He had other things on his mind.

He had decided to ask her to marry him during their last night at the beach. He asked at the hotel desk and was told, "Well, the best restaurant with a beach view is the Mad Hatter on Sanibel, but I'm not supposed to say that. I'm supposed to tell you the restaurant next door is." He called and made a reservation at the Mad Hatter for Saturday so they could have a window seat and be there at sunset.

They spent their last day on the beach, walking and talking. At least, Amanda talked. Cutter was distracted. Distant. "Is something wrong?"

"Oh. No. No. Everything is terrific. I guess I'm just sorry to see the vacation end. This has been great. Thinking about what I'm going to do when we get back to the Cities."

"What do you mean, 'do'?" she wondered.

"About work. I guess it's about time for me to get a big boy job. Full time. Wear a tie. You know. Join the adult world." He wanted her to know he could be responsible. Husbandly. More importantly, fatherly.

After afternoon naps, they got ready for dinner. She wore her Mumu style print dress; he wore his brand new pink Hawaiian shirt and black cargo shorts. They drove out to Sanibel and, since they had arrived early, they drove up through Captiva and marveled at the wealth. They both agreed they would live there some day. He took that as a good sign.

Back to the restaurant. They had to wait for their table. He was nervous. Not because he was under dressed. Though realizing that did not help. She was excited. She got to have her weekly glass of wine tonight. She had saved it for just such an occasion. Finally they were seated, studied the menu (Jesus, this is pretty fucking expensive) and ordered. They waited for their dinner.

"Amanda," he said, taking her hand.

"Yes?"

"I love you." Wow, he'd said it. Just like that. He'd said it. Maybe this wouldn't be too hard. Maybe this will be great.

"I know. I love you too. I don't know how I would have made it through all of this without you. You have been so good to me. The best friend I have ever had."

Now was the time. Ask her.

He looked at her smiling face. But what he saw was not the face that had been in the photograph Terry had taken. This was a friendly face. Not an in-love face. He flashed on Tommie's face. We can't get married. You're just a boy.

"Yes?" Amanda asked, trying to figure out what was going on.

"Nothing. I just wanted to tell you I love you."

Their dinner came. They talked about what a fun week it had been. How they hated to go back. Watched the sunset, which they agreed was the best they had ever seen. Walked hand in hand on the beach after, him drinking a bourbon, her a club soda. Drove back to the hotel.

Later that night, after they were in bed, Amanda said, "Cutter, you awake?"

"Yep."

"Thanks. Thank you so much for everything."

"You bet. My pleasure."

On the plane the next day, Cutter stared out the window, watching Fort Myers Beach and Sanibel slide away. Amanda wanted to know, "So you were a boy scout, huh?"

He kept his eyes on the coastline, "Nope."

TWELVE

Clint filled a new glass with bourbon and sat down at the table where Cutter was writing on his laptop. Drank half the bourbon in one swallow.

"You all right?" Cutter asked. "You look like shit."

"Yeah. Yeah. I'm fine. I think I need some air," Clint answered. He got up and walked up to the main deck, Cutter staring at his back as he left.

What the fuck am I going to do? Cat crap and apple butter. Wow. Odd time for my grandmother to slip out. Double fuck. Grandma would never have said that. Triple fuck. How could Sandy do this? Doesn't she get it? I can't let it all come apart. There has to be an answer. Triple fuck fudge sundae. If I tell the guys, how can I make sure Lynn never finds out? Never? Why would I care about never? Lynn. Shit.

When Clint went to work at the chamber of commerce, he was a year out of college and took the first thing they offered him. Which was in technical support. Here he was, the future President of the United States, basically a glorified AV guy. Just like the lowest of the dweebs in high school. But it did bring him in contact with everyone in the organization and meant he got to go to big meetings and trade shows, so it wasn't all bad.

He had been there about a year when his job required him to set up and run the technical side of the chamber's huge "Do Business in Davenport" display at the annual Iowa Business Fair held in Des Moines. The Davenport contingent included the chamber president, the two vice presidents and the chairman of the chamber's board, the managing partner of the area's biggest law firm. And the summer intern, a college junior. Who just happened to be the daughter of the chairman of the board. The intern, Lynn French, was terrific looking and apparently pretty smart, but she acted like having to deal with the low lifes who worked at the chamber was way beneath her. Clint knew how she felt, though he didn't like being considered a low life by her.

He had to drive the equipment van with the display to Des Moines, while the rest of them rode in the chamber's hulking SUV. He didn't really mind, though. He had some tunes and mostly he didn't have to listen to the two vice presidents try to one up each other in front of the bosses. And it amused him that Lynn would have to sit through all that while her father was right there. In fact, it made him laugh out loud every time he thought about it.

The show was pretty standard and, as usual, manning the booth was a boring pain in the ass. Smile, hand out literature, smile again. The bosses, that is, the two underling bosses, took turns being the spokesperson at the booth. Lynn also got to smile and hand out literature. They did get to talk. Turned out she wasn't the complete bitch he thought she was. In fact, the second night in town, they even went to dinner together. She spent a lot of time name dropping. Talking about brand shopping. Whining about having to work. He didn't mind. She was nice to look at. He noticed that other people paid attention to them as a couple. Yeah, we do look pretty good together.

The evening they left to return to Davenport, Lynn volunteered to ride with Clint. Mr. French thought that was a sweet thing for his daughter to offer, "Sure, Lynn, it would be nice if you would keep, uh, uh, this young man company. I'm sorry. I forgot your name."

"Clint Brandsgard, sir," Clint offered.

"Oh, yeah, Clint."

Clint was happy to have her along. And he was going to get a lot happier. Half an hour out of Des Moines on I-80, Lynn pulled a box from the back, put it next to the driver's seat and sat down. Put her hand on Clint's leg and her head on his shoulder. Ten minutes after that, Clint had his arm around her and was all the way to second base. Which she seemed to enjoy immensely. Gave him the courage to steal third. Safe. Of course, a guy can't slide home when he's driving. Still, the drive back was becoming a lot more fun than the drive over.

Lynn was intent. And not finished. She unzipped

him and put her head in his lap. He was able to concentrate enough to keep the van between the white lines, but not enough to keep up speed. As she finished, his cell phone rang. She giggled. He looked at the phone. It was his boss, calling from the SUV way out in front of them. He answered, "Hello?" His voice husky.

"Is everything okay? You've slowed way down," his boss asked.

Clint snapped to, "Yeah. We just had a little overheating problem, but things are fine now."

Lynn giggled again.

They went out almost every night for the month before she returned to college in Madison. Initially her father was not too excited about his daughter dating AV guy, but he asked around about the kid and decided Clint might just have a future. Lynn's mother loved Clint. Clint loved them all. Her dad because he was rich and powerful and could be a help. Her mom because she fawned and gushed all over him. Lynn because she was so incredible in bed. She would do anything, and more importantly, anything he did drove her wild. Made him feel like super stud. And she looked very good standing next to him.

He drove up to Madison every weekend she didn't come home. At Christmas, they got engaged. June wedding. Because of her dad, all of the Quad Cities was in attendance. At least all of the important people. Great wedding gifts, including a house from her parents. The down payment anyway. Clint and Lynn had to pay the mortgage. Which wasn't too difficult because, surprise, surprise, Clint had just gotten a big promotion at the chamber, over more senior coworkers. He was now chief of all business communications. Those things settled, Clint got on with the business of becoming President. Of the United States.

All went according to plan. Except for the little hiccup with the bank lady. Lynn had been pissed. Made him move out. Had herself a fling with the owner of the art gallery where she worked part time. Made sure Clint knew about it. Decided she was risking her shot at being First Lady so she let him come home. With the understanding that if he ever cheated again, she was going to cut off his balls with a rusty razor blade.

And now this. Clint shook off those thoughts and summoned Clint the Soldier. Not the little one that had caused this problem. The big one, who would fix it. You can't win the war if you don't fight the battle. You can't fight the battle if you don't have a solid battle plan. Time for a call to arms. He bounded downstairs, and ordered Cutter, "Get Pat and Ken and meet me in the wheelhouse up top. Now. And do it quietly."

"Sandy, too?" Cutter asked.

"No!" A little too forceful. "Come on, Cutter, move it."

Cutter sure didn't know what was going on, but it wasn't a tone Clint had ever used with him before. Cutter had heard that tone, but it was usually reserved for lazy or obstructionist bureaucrats. Before Cutter could respond, Clint had disappeared up through the hatch.

Up top, Clint threw the door to the wheelhouse open and scared the shit out of Jordair, who had just settled in for his watch and was reading the book *A Confederacy of Dunces*. "What's wrong?" Jordair demanded.

"Nothing. Sorry I startled you," Clint answered. "Could we use this cabin for a little while?" he wondered.

"Sure. I guess so. But I have to stay in here. I can't leave my post. It's illegal and I would lose my job."

"Oh. Well, shit." Clint thought for a second. "Is there any other private place I could meet with my guys for a few minutes? I mean, besides down below?"

"Uh, no, not really. But if you don't want me to hear something, I could put on my headphones and turn up the music. As long as I can see the instrument panel and the ocean, I'm fine. Just let me know if you hear anything loud or unusual, okay?"

"That would be terrific. Thanks, Jordair, you're a life saver," Clint smiled his campaign smile as the others walked in. Looking grim.

"So what's this about?" Pat wanted to know.

Clint kept the campaign smile on his face. "Oh, a bit of a snag has come up. But nothing I'm sure you guys can't fix."

Concerned looks around. Well, Pat and Cutter looked concerned. Ken just looked confused. Stared into his glass of bourbon.

Clint turned to Jordair and said politely, "Do you mind?"

"Oh. Yeah. Sorry." With that Jordair reached into

a bin and pulled out a set of large headphones, plugged them into the console and turned the music up high enough that the others could hear it faintly. Went back to his book.

Now Pat was clearly irritated. "What's this all about, Clint? Pull us up here in the middle of the night, do this secret spy stuff. What the hell is going on?"

Clint looked dead serious. Maybe a little afraid.

"I'm sorry guys. But I've fucked up. Seriously fucked up. This is a 'no tell'. Understood?"

They all knew what that meant. "No tell" was a Clint Brandsgard absolute. If he, or anyone of them, said this to anyone else in the group, and the listener agreed, then it was mutually understood that whatever it was stayed between the two of them. You were not allowed to tell anyone, any time, even if they were in the group. Even if they were in your bed. The punishment was exile. Two years earlier a young aide who was quickly on his way to becoming one of the chosen shared a no tell with his wife and it got back to Clint. The guy was now counting tires in the city garage, wondering what the hell had happened.

Ken and Pat nodded their heads. Understood. Cutter was not so sure. Clint assumed that Cutter had agreed by his silence.

"Sandy's pregnant." Clint told them.

Ken, "I don't get it. Isn't that good news? How does that screw things up?"

"It's mine," Clint admitted.

"Oh, sweet Jesus," moaned Pat and he slumped

back into his seat. "How the hell could you do that? Are you a fucking idiot? Haven't we been through this kind of shit enough? Clint, you are beyond hope. I'm fucking quitting." He had kept his eye on the wrong Guinevere. But he didn't make any move toward leaving.

Ken dropped his glass on the floor and the motion caught Jordair's eye, which made him start. Jordair turned to see what was going on and Clint patted the air toward him to let him know it was nothing.

Cutter just shook his head. How could his friend do this? To another friend? Testosterone and vaginas. A bad combination. Always had been, always would be. And the more testosterone there was, the worse it got. The headlines were always full of it. The richer, the more powerful, the more famous a man became, somehow it increased his testosterone level. That attracted more vaginas. And vice versa. It took a special person to see it for what it was and resist it. Apparently neither Clint nor Sandy was that special. Christ in a hand basket.

"So what's going to happen?" Cutter asked.

"That's what we have to figure out. The four of us," Clint answered.

"What the fuck do you mean, 'figure out'," Cutter fired back. "This isn't our problem. It's yours. And Sandy's. But if you are asking me, I think you should do the right thing. Get divorced. Marry her."

"It's not that simple, Cutter. Right now that would put all we've worked for at risk. The obvious answer is for her to have an abortion. No harm, no foul. But she doesn't want to do that. She wants to have this baby. I love her, but what kind of future would any of us have?"

"Future? You should have fucking thought about that earlier. You can't force her to have an abortion," Cutter countered, angry. Very angry.

Pat interceded, "Wait a minute, Cutter. Don't be so righteous. Maybe we can fix this. We hold all the cards. Sandy will just have to understand it is the only good option. Sure, she can have the kid and even prove it's Clint's. But not until after the election. The court would probably order support, but we could avoid that public scene by having Kenny negotiate a settlement," Pat was warming to the idea that Merlin might just be able to work some magic.

Pat continued, "If she lets it come out, she would be ruined. Paul will divorce her. We can put it all on her. She seduced the mayor to increase her power. It was all a set up. She gets shunned. Who will listen to her? We all know how smart she is and that all the good ideas have been hers, but no one else knows. She is just that woman in the background of photos. Forgotten by the time the governor's race comes around."

He finished, "Yeah, I think Sandy will see that getting rid of it is her only good choice. Ken here can sell her on that. I'm sure of it." He waved his arm around, Merlin waving his magic wand.

Ken finally found his voice, "I don't think I can do that, Pat. Especially if I'm going to be involved legally later. I think this is something Clint and Sandy have to work out between themselves." It was the most serious Cutter had ever seen Ken.

Pat's eyes narrowed and he looked from Ken to Cutter and back again. "I don't think you two get this. Do you realize where Mr. Brandsgard is going to take us all? I mean truly understand? The statehouse is a forgone conclusion, but the governor's office is just a jumping off place to go national. I'm talking about a presidential run in twelve years. There is no one out there on the horizon right now who has the upside potential that Clint has." Clint was now smiling. "We can't let this little thing side track us. Either Sandy goes with us, or she is left behind. Remember, this situation is as much her fault as Clint's. Probably more." It hadn't taken Pat long to paint Sandy as the criminal here. It fit his needs better.

Clint, serious again, "I don't know. Sandy seemed pretty intent on not having an abortion. I don't want her to get hurt." But Cutter didn't hear any sincerity in his voice. Plainly, Clint wanted someone to take this off of him.

Christ in a hand basket.

Pat took over. "This has to be handled before we get back to shore." To Clint, "Does Lynn know?"

"Oh for God's sake, no. And she can't know. She would raise hell, a hell none of us can afford. You know Lynn. She is mostly oblivious, but when she gets pissed, 'scorn' takes on a whole new meaning."

Pat went on, "Somebody has to talk to Sandy. Obviously, it can't be Clint. Ken has a good point about the legal side. She doesn't trust me. That leaves you, Cutter. You have to talk with her. She likes you. Trusts you. While we are still on the boat. You have to get her to agree."

"Pat, let me say this as plainly as I can. Fuck you. And fuck the horse you rode in on. And all the little horses' asses that would come from that union. But if you like, I would be more than happy to talk to Lynn. I would love seeing her face." Cutter wasn't kidding.

Pat barked at him, "Fine, Cutter. You're out of it. All of it. I'll do it myself." He stood up to leave.

Cutter said, "Wait. Wait a minute." After his outburst, he had thought about it. It would be better if he talked to her. Much better. "I'll do it. I'll talk to her. But not tonight. In the morning. I need to think this through. What I can say to her."

Clint said quietly, "Thank you, Cutter. I really mean it. I won't forget this."

"No you won't, Clint Brandsgard. No you won't." thought Cutter.

They were both right.

THIRTEEN

"Cutter? Cutter!"

"Huh. What?" He opened one eye.

"Cutter, I think it's time."

"Time for what?" Still not awake.

"Time to go to the hospital. I'm in labor," Amanda said, a look on her face that was somewhere between relief and concern.

Five seconds later the idea penetrated Cutter's brain. Two seconds after that, Cutter was up pulling on his jeans, eyes flashing. "Okay. I'm ready. Let's go," he moved toward the door.

Now Amanda smiled. "Not yet. We have time for coffee and breakfast. Well, you can have breakfast. I better not eat. The contractions are still fifteen minutes apart."

"These aren't those hickey things, are they?" Cutter wanted to know. He couldn't remember the name of Braxton Hicks contractions. Amanda had had those a week before and they got ready to go to the hospital then.

"No, Cutter, I think this is the real thing. I called

the doctor and he told me to go in when the contractions were eight to ten minutes apart. Go take your shower and I'll make you some eggs and toast."

Cutter padded down the hall to the bathroom, noticed Amanda had a bag packed in the hallway and that she had already spent some time in the bathroom. He wondered how long she had been awake. He showered, shaved, dressed and got to the kitchen as Amanda was buttering his toast. He saw the kitchen was sparkling, not the total mess they had left when they fell into bed last night. She must have been up for a while.

She had two more contractions before they left, both lasting under a minute. She appeared to Cutter to be in a lot of pain, but she waved him back, panted for a while, then relaxed, telling him it was nothing. After breakfast, she cleaned the kitchen and did one more house check to assure herself she had done everything. Cutter was getting anxious, wanted her to move it along. Finally they were in his Camry, on the way to the hospital.

As soon as they were on their way out of the Heights, Amanda laid her hand on Cutter's. "Cutter, if I don't get a chance again today to tell you, thank you for everything. I couldn't have gone through this without you. I can't go through this without you." With that, Amanda had another contraction and stiffened to the point that her finger nails dug into the back of Cutter's hand and drew blood. He immediately pulled over and let her work her way through the contraction.

"You ready to move again?" he asked. Her eyes were closed and she was motionless.

"Can we sit here for a few minutes?" she asked quietly, eyes still closed.

"No problem. Anything you want me to do?"

"No." She took a couple of deep breaths. "And thank you for being so understanding. About everything."

Cutter chuckled. She opened her eyes, "Did I say something funny?"

He was still smiling, his aw shucks smile. "Yeah, you did. Truth is, Amanda, I don't understand at all. The way you think. The way women operate. Oh, I get the whole boys play with balls and trucks; girls play with dolls and horses. Men hunt and fish and women shop. Men never tell each other anything; women tell each other everything. I get those differences, but I can't begin to fathom how you all think."

"Oh, Cutter, don't be a ninny. You…"

He cut her off. "I'm serious here. I even get some of the rules. Like when a woman complains about something, she doesn't want a man to fix it for her. She just wants him to listen and empathize. But beyond that, I am hopelessly lost. In college I read a book, Chopin's *The Awakening*. I remember thinking at the time, there is something going on here, beyond what I get, that only a female would get. I never got it. The same is true now. I love you. But understanding? Nope. That I don't got."

She started to spasm again. She smiled at him weakly and said, "I think we better move." He did.

At the hospital, the staff put Amanda in a wheel chair and took her away, instructing Cutter where to park the car and where to bring her bag. Twenty minutes later they were in a room, Amanda in bed, talking while they waited for the next contraction. That was to be the pattern for the next ten hours. Sometimes there would be just two minutes between contractions, sometimes up to fifteen. It seemed to Cutter to be taking forever, but the doctors assured them both things were going fine. So he fed her ice chips and popsicles, rubbed her back and kept her company.

At about eight in the evening, Amanda experienced a particularly intense and lengthy contraction, enough to make Cutter go find a nurse. By the time he returned with the nurse, the contraction had ended, but there was blood on the sheets. Not a lot, but any was a bad sign. Cutter knew that. He immediately started asking questions as the doctor entered but was told he would have to leave the room for a while. He squeezed Amanda's hand, kissed her on the cheek and left the room. He realized as he was walking out that it was the first time he had ever kissed her.

He wandered down to the cafeteria and got coffee and a sandwich. Returned to the floor and was told to wait in the waiting room on the floor below. He did as instructed. He sat and watched reruns of old TV shows. Sat some more. On a hard plastic chair. Divided his time between staring at the faded blue wall and checking the large clock whose monotonous ticking became more and more irritating.

At midnight he went back up to the floor Amanda was on and found that the staff at the nurses' station had all changed. He asked the large woman at the desk about Amanda.

"I'm sorry sir. Are you a member of the family?"

"No, but I..." Cutter started to explain, but she cut him off.

"I'm sorry, sir, but we can only share information with members of the family." With that the nurse turned away and intently concentrated on the computer monitor with her back to Cutter.

Cutter tried again, "Uh, yeah, I'm Amanda's cousin and we are very close, so I need to talk with someone about her. I am her coach and should be with her."

The nurse kept her back to Cutter, "Go back down to the waiting room and someone will be with you." Cutter did as he was told and stared at the wall and the clock some more. After an hour, he finally figured out she had been lying to him to get him to leave. He stormed back up to the floor above. A new receptionist was at the desk. He tried again, this time, telling the young girl that he was Amanda's brother. She consulted her computer monitor and said, "Gee, there must be some mix up. Her records don't indicate that she has a brother."

Damn, how could I forget that? Christ in a hand basket. "I don't know what the records say, but can you please, oh, please, tell me what's going on with her?"

The receptionist smiled and told him, "Let me find the doctor and he can talk to you. Just wait downstairs and he'll be with you in a few minutes." He knew he would never see any doctor down there, but he went back anyway. He was angry. And very tired. I'll just close my eyes for a few minutes. Just a few.

He woke several hours later, every muscle and bone in his body hurting. He went to the bathroom and looked in the mirror on the way out. He was a mess. Hair even worse than usual, eyes bloodshot, needing a shave. Breath that would down a horse. He did the best to control the damage with soap, water, and a breath mint, found a cup of coffee and tried again to get information. A whole new group of nurses. The new receptionist asked him to have a seat right there. That was a good sign. Two minutes later, a young doctor collected Cutter and took him aside.

"Mr. Williams, Amanda asked me to tell you that she and the baby are both all right." Cutter relaxed so much he actually started to fall. The doctor caught him and made him sit down before continuing. "As you may have guessed, there were complications, and it was touch and go for a while. But everything worked out and she is resting comfortably now. Her parents are with her."

Her parents? What the fuck were they doing here? All this time, they ignore her and then ride in at the last minute. "Her parents are here?" Cutter said, clearly confused.

"Oh, yes, we called them last night when things

weren't going well. They drove right down to be with her. They said to tell you 'thanks' and they will handle things from here." Cutter was so astounded and angry he couldn't speak. The doctor excused himself and walked away.

Cutter said to his back, "Wait a minute. What was it? The baby, I mean."

The doctor turned and smiled, "A little girl. Healthy and beautiful."

"Can I see them? Amanda and the baby."

"Sorry, the parents don't want Amanda disturbed right now. I'm sure they'll let you know when you can see her."

They didn't. Which didn't surprise Cutter in the least. He was part of Amanda's "unpleasantness" and would be relegated to *persona non grata* status. Cutter drove home, called the ad agency to tell them he was taking a couple more days off, got drunk on half of a bottle of bourbon and slept for twelve hours.

Over the next couple of days he tried to call her several times but always ended up in voice mail. She finally texted him to tell him she was fine, in Dubuque and would call him when she got back to the Quad Cities. Nothing about the baby. Nothing.

Two weeks later, he came home and found her sitting on his front stoop. When he got out of his car, she jumped up and ran down to him, throwing her arms around him, holding on for dear life. He hugged her in return and they stood there, not speaking, holding each other for several minutes. Finally he let go, took her shoulders in his hands and held her at arms' length. She looked so small, back to her original hundred and ten pounds, soaking wet, size. She started to speak, had a catch in her voice that sounded a bit like a sob, then started over, "Cutter. Winston Weller Williams. It is so good to see you. I've missed you terribly. Can we have dinner? Are you busy? Am I interrupting your plans?" It was like listening to a machine gun try to talk.

"Nothing I can't cancel," he replied. In fact he had nothing planned at all, but for some reason, as happy as he was to see her, he still felt lots of anger. Nothing for weeks and now she is back like nothing has happened. Why is she back? Cutter had thought long and hard about it. She of course would have to move on. They would have, he hoped, a good bye, but he saw it as a formal, "Goodbye. Thank you. Have a nice life. Hope everything works out for you," slightly awkward goodbye. Not this. Not this "I'm back and happy and let's get dinner," greeting.

Even though it was fall, it was still warm. "Let's go to the Boat House and you can finally buy me that beer you promised me a long time ago," she chirped.

"Okay." Fifteen minutes later they were on the deck of the restaurant, watching the barges loaded with grain head downriver. As they walked in, Amanda ordered two beers, remembering Cutter's aversion to making beer choices. Within seconds of their sitting down, two very large beers were set in front of them. She picked up her mug and held it out toward him, "A toast to the best friend a girl could have."

Cutter was a little embarrassed. He touched her mug with his and said, "Thanks."

"I didn't mean you. I meant the beer," and laughed at her own jibe. "So I suppose you want an explanation. Of what happened, I mean."

"Yeah, that would be nice. You did, after all, leave me kind of dangling in the breeze at the hospital, you know."

"I know. And I am sorry. I didn't have a lot of control over the situation." With that she launched into the story of those hours he stared at the blue wall and worried. The bleeding had been bad, much worse than they first thought. The doctors moved her to another room and set up an IV and sedated her. Called her parents because they were not sure she was going to survive. They got the hemorrhaging stopped and decided to do a C-section. Put her to sleep. Woke her back up to show her the baby and she managed to tell them to send him a message that she was okay, though she never heard if he got it. She went back under the knife and woke up a day and a half later. By then, child welfare had taken her baby and she was scheduled to go to court the next day to finalize the adoption. When she heard she would not see the child again, she kind of lost it and they sedated her again. The next day her father took her to court. Her memory of that was very foggy. The next thing she knew she was waking up in her old bedroom in Dubuque.

"Cutter, I can't begin to explain my emotions. I wanted to talk to you, but I was angry at you and everyone else. I didn't, still don't, know why. I just couldn't face you...even if it was just on the phone. I let my mom take care of me. They told my sister I had had an operation and come home to recover. I wasn't allowed to talk about any of it. I cried. Every day. For long periods of time. And then I just got cried out."

"The doctor in Dubuque released me and I came home this morning. I'm going back to work next week. Get to see that fucking Fenton. And my kids."

From Cutter, nothing.

"Well?" she wanted to know. "Don't you have anything to say?"

"I missed you. I really thought I would never see you or hear from you again. I'm happy you're back." He was.

She got up and came to his side of the table, leaned down and kissed him, for the first time, and announced, "I'm hungry. Starved. Famished. Feed me."

Cutter bought her the steak just the way she ordered it, "If it's frozen, thaw it. If it's thawed, serve it."

FOURTEEN

Cutter woke up angry. He couldn't remember why he was angry, but his first thought was to rip someone's head off. Did I have a bad dream? Did I have the dream again? No. Not it. Oh, Christ in a hand basket. Fucking Clint. Truly asshole Pat. What can I possibly say to Sandy? How are we going to get out of this mess? Fuck.

He lay for a moment, looking at the polished wood ceiling over his bed and felt the boat rocking with the swells. He slowly became aware of the noises from the deck and the smell of bacon. It was enough to rouse him. Into the head, then pulled on his swimming trunks and went top side.

"Morning, Jordair."

"Hey, Cutter, how's it hanging? Looked like you guys were really going at it last night. Everything okay?" Jordair wondered.

"Yeah. Yeah. Just fine." Cutter lied. "Is it okay to take a little swim out here?"

"Sure. But do us a favor and wear a life jacket."

Cutter pulled on a jacket and cinched it, turned,

and as he jumped in, heard Jordair yell, "Watch out for the sharks," and then laugh. "Well fuck," thought Cutter, "why is it no one ever warns me about sharks 'til it's too late?" The water was colder than he had expected, so he swam around enough to get the salt and grime from yesterday off his skin and his muscles working and then he pulled himself up the ladder on the back of the boat.

Jordair, still smiling, said, "Go get some breakfast and then back up here. I'll have a rig set up in a few minutes and you can jump in the chair before anyone else gets here. This is the best time to catch a sailfish, you know."

"Thanks. And thanks for the shark warning. Scared the shit out of me," Cutter replied as he headed down to the galley. There he found Samantha and Sandy. Both smiled and greeted him, Sandy with a suggestive, "Hey, sailor." It took a second of confusion before Cutter worked out that while he knew and Sandy knew, Sandy didn't know that he knew. Good. I'm not ready for that yet.

"You want some eggs and bacon? Scrambled okay?" Samantha asked.

"Gee, I really had my heart set on bluefish, but eggs and bacon will do," Cutter deadpanned. To Sandy, "Hey, Jordair is setting me up to fish first, but I was wondering if afterwards you would have some time to go over some things on your proposal. I have some questions." Great. I talk to three people this morning and lie to all of them. Gonna be a great fucking day.

"You bet. Whenever you're ready." How could she be so chipper? Swear to God, I will never figure women out. Complex beyond any reasonable definition of functionality.

Yeah, Sandy was complex, but she would argue about the beyond functionality part. And not just because she liked to argue. Which she did. If it was an intellectual argument. Emotional arguments she wasn't too fond of. It was the way she was trained. More precisely, forced to be.

She was the youngest of four children and the sole girl. Three older brothers, boys raised to be star athletes, and to varying degrees, successful at it. Father prized athleticism, the benefits of team play and stoicism. Oh, and thought that a woman's place was in the home there in Mason City, feeding, cleaning and caring for young athletes and the grand men athletics turned them into. Little women grew into capable big women by helping their mothers take care of men. Since she knew no other life, Sandy was fine with the arrangement, though she quietly wished that washing dishes garnered the same accolades as kicking a goal or scoring a basket. She also wished that her father would hug her sometimes. Wished it weren't so unmanly.

Sandy flourished in school. The more she studied, the more she paid attention, the more she participated in class, the more praise she got. Her mom even seemed to like her doing well in school. Though when she came home and announced she was trying out for soccer, her mother told her that proper little girls didn't play sports; when she was older she could be a cheerleader.

Turned out serious, shy, plain girls didn't get selected as cheerleaders. She joined color guard, the group of girls (and one very strange boy named Jacob) who ran around with the band at football games, throwing flags and fake swords and fake guns in the air. Which was okay with mom and dad. Probably because they didn't realize that the other side of color guard was drill team, a highly competitive, ultra athletic sport. Her parents never came to her competitions nor saw the crowds cheer when she did routines no one had ever done before. She loved the applause. It felt like, well, like acceptance.

She got a full academic scholarship to the University of Iowa where she majored in business administration. Her father approved. Thought it might help her get a job as an administrative assistant to some man doing important work. As it went, that is what it got her. Didn't hurt that somewhere in her college career she had also turned into quite a looker. Except the work wasn't important in her eyes. It was just about turning lots of money into even more money. She was hired as an assistant to an assistant to Gerald Huntsman. Being an assistant was not what she wanted, but it paid her well enough that she didn't have to go back to Mason City. She had learned things in college which, frankly, made the prospect of going home disgusting.

Another of Mr. Huntsman's myriad assistants, Paul Morton, was quick to notice this attractive addition to the staff and, since he was the number one minion, managed to get her reassigned to a work area near him. Now he could pursue her as if she were a new business opportunity. Sandy, for her part, was quite taken with the attention of this older, powerful man. Not just business dominant, but physically powerful. He had wrestled as a heavyweight for Iowa State. He was a mesomorph who wore his masculinity like a crown.

Paul lavished attention on her, took her places, introduced her to people, listened to her every word, held every door open for her. Swept her off her feet. Her parents loved Paul. Especially her dad. He proposed. She accepted. The big wedding, the grand tour honeymoon. A new house, which she got to furnish. One month after they returned from their honeymoon, Paul asked her to quit her job. She wasn't sure about it, but because he had asked, she quit. She became one of the ladies who lunch. She took up tennis. Spent time at the country club. Shopped. Tried to get pregnant.

Couldn't. She went to the doctor. She was fine. Paul went. He wasn't. He could never father children. He seemed fine with it. Didn't really want to share his life with kids anyway. She was lost. Seemed to float along. She had opinions, thoughts, good thoughts. Paul didn't seem to care. Then the mayor asked her opinion and she found herself. New job. Making a difference in others' lives, in her life. Then she fell in love. Something she discovered she had never done before, not really. All that time she had tried to get pregnant. Now she was. It may not be convenient, but Clint loved her and in her heart of hearts, she knew it would work out.

"So what do you really think of the proposal?" Sandy asked Cutter.

"I think it is incredible. So simple, everyone looks right by it. No one cannot be supportive," he replied. She grinned ear to ear.

"Thanks. I'm pretty excited," she added.

"You wouldn't be if you knew how your coworkers were talking about you," he thought, but only said, "Me, too."

As Cutter finished his eggs and got another cup of coffee, Lynn and Clint made their grand entrance into the dining room. "Good morning, troops. Another fine day to be at sea, eh," Clint once again using his campaign voice.

"Good morning," from Sandy; "Morning, sir," from Samantha.

Cutter rose and walked out without a word. Even Lynn noticed. "What's bugging the twerp?" she wanted to know.

"Ah, you know how Cutter is in the morning. You can't talk to him until noon," offered Clint.

Sandy added, "Don't know. He seemed fine a few minutes ago."

By this time, Cutter was in the Hemingway chair and Jordair had the *Debbie Lee* trolling four lines, all big rigs. Cutter was drinking his coffee and watching the sun bounce off the ocean surface. He was deep in thought when Jordair interrupted him by handing him a rod, "Cutter, wake up. I think this may be the real deal."

"What?" Before Jordair could answer, Cutter felt the full force of the fish on the other end of the line. "Whoa! I see what you mean," Cutter was fighting back and holding on for dear life. Jordair belted him into the seat and cleared the other lines from the water. Within minutes, Cutter's mind was cleared of everything except that fish. How it pulled and strained, how it would seem to disappear, only to surge back with a force that would have yanked Cutter into the water had he not been strapped in. Cutter alternately reeled in and let the fish run out. Jordair stood by him, doing a little coaching, but pretty much let Cutter work the fish on his own.

Jordair told him, "Pretty soon it will probably break the surface, trying to throw the line. Be ready and don't try to reel in or pull when he does. Let him have the slack he needs. Let him tire himself out." But the fish didn't break the surface. It just kept diving, rising and zigzagging.

The battle was on. The fish tried to go under the boat, use it as protection. Captain Jefferson countered and when the fish was back in open water, brought the *Debbie Lee* around so Cutter would not be staring into the morning sun. The activity brought all hands on deck. Not Samantha, who was cleaning up breakfast, nor Pat, who was locked in his cabin, plotting, but everyone else. Clint was drinking coffee, Lynn and Ken were already into the Bloody Marys and lemonade for

Sandy, who offered some to Cutter. Everyone was excited and happy, save Ken who was morose. Lynn and Sandy assumed it was because either he was hung over or Samantha had shot him down big time. Clint and Cutter knew why but ignored it.

After forty minutes, Cutter was cursing himself for not using that free gym membership that was a perk of his job. Made a promise to himself to start going at least three times a week. Course, that wouldn't help him now and he was getting tired. But it took another forty-five minutes before the fight went out of the fish. At first, Cutter thought he had lost it. But when he started reeling, he realized there was still a huge weight on the other end. Slowly and steadily he brought the fish closer to the boat. The line must have extended three hundred yards into the ocean.

Jordair grabbed a gaff and got to the stern, everybody crowding around him to see Cutter's fish. As it came to the surface, Jordair whispered, "Son of a bitch. I don't believe it," and then said louder, "Everyone please stand back." They all took two steps backward. With that he flung the fish onto the deck. All ninety pounds, eight and a half feet of what appeared to them to be nothing more than a huge mouth filled with the biggest, sharpest teeth they had ever seen—a barracuda. They all jumped back as far and fast as they could. Even Cutter tried to move away, though he was restrained and all he could do was lift his feet and throw down the pole.

The huge fish flopped around on the deck, the teeth slashing all directions. Jordair jumped to avoid the teeth, opened a cabinet and pulled out what looked to Cutter like the biggest handgun ever made by man. When he realized that Jordair was going to shoot the fish and probably blow a hole in the bottom of the boat, he tried to scream, "Stop!" but his word was drowned out by the explosion. Ah, shit. Absolute dead quiet as the fish flopped two more times and came to a rest, all of its teeth showing.

Jordair grinned. He turned to a wild-eyed Cutter who looked stunned. "Not to worry, Cutter. It shoots hard wax bullets. If it hits the deck, it just flattens out. No hole, no ricochet. Didn't want that barracuda cutting us to ribbons."

Captain Jefferson joined them and patted, first Jordair and then Cutter, and said, "Good job, men. Nasty fish, that. But it looks to be near record size."

Everyone edged in to get a better look at it. Ken had gone from morose to impressed and wanted another drink. Went to get one for himself and Cutter as well. Cutter asked them, "What do we do with it? Have it stuffed? Can we eat it?"

Captain Jefferson shook his head and said, "I don't think so. Apparently some are poisonous to eat. Maybe mount it—if you have the money to spend. We'll haul it back for measurement. You may have a record fish there."

Cutter looked at the big deadly and dead fish and suddenly knew what he would say to Sandy. He peeled off his shirt, shed his shoes and jumped into the water. It felt great. Everyone stood at the stern and applauded. He got out, someone handed him a towel and Ken handed him a drink. He dried off, turned to Sandy and said, "Let's go up front and talk." She nodded yes and Cutter noticed Clint relax and smile.

When they were lying on towels on the fore deck, Cutter said to her, "I need you to listen for a few minutes and not react. Okay?"

She nodded an uncertain okay.

"Clint told us." It took a few seconds for it to sink in. Her shoulders stiffened, her face hardened. Then she smiled and said softly, "Good."

Cutter continued, "No. Not good. Decidedly not good." Her smile was gone. She started to speak and he held up his hand. "Listen to me. Don't say a word until I am done. I have thought all night about what I could say to you. What 'they' want me to say to you. I have decided to report to you, as accurately as I can, exactly what was said and who said it. Then we'll discuss it if you wish."

"Cutter, this is all going to work out. I love Clint and he loves me. It may be difficult but it will all work out. I promise."

"Listen. Please not another word until I finish." He told her, word for word, the conversation from last night. As best he could recall, realizing his memory was clouded by anger. She shook her head violently, looked confused and hurt and angry, but she said nothing. When he finished, she stared at him, tears in her eyes.

"I don't believe it. Clint loves me. I love him. He will do what he promised to do."

144

"What did he actually promise?" She was mute. "Did he make you a campaign promise? Something that would happen after he is elected?"

"Cutter, you don't understand. We love each other. Love can fix these things."

"I'm sorry, I don't believe that. I don't believe love fixes anything." He then told her the story of Amanda. Including their last chapter.

FIFTEEN

Cutter and Amanda settled into a routine, not much different than the one they had been in before. She spent time at his apartment, he at hers. She taught and talked about her kids constantly and that fucking Fenton less constantly. She would kiss him, apparently with passion, but she stopped everything else. No touching, no I love you's. Cutter figured, correctly, that she was trying to find her way. She mostly wanted him around, to fill the space. He was a comfort. She needed comfort.

"Hey, Cutter, you want to go up to Dubuque with me this weekend? Meet my family. It's my birthday."

Christ in a hand basket, how could he not know when her birthday was. Was he that oblivious?

"Sure. That would be great. I'd love to meet your family," he told her, though he was still pissed at them for the way they treated him when the baby was born.

"You'll have to stay in the guestroom. I hope that is okay."

"No problem."

They drove up Friday evening and arrived in time

for a late dinner. Introductions all around, Cutter introduced as "a friend". Amanda's little sister announced to everyone that she thought Cutter was cute. Polite laughter. Conversation around the table was in low tones and with little energy. No jokes. No plays on words. Certainly no *double entendres*. They talked about Amanda's work and her sister's school. They asked about his job, they listened and then said, "Ah. Sounds like interesting work." Bullshit. Most of it was boring.

After dinner, Amanda's father invited Cutter into his den to share an after dinner drink. How terribly gentlemen's club of him. Cutter figured he couldn't decline. Although what he really wanted to do was grab Amanda, drag her out of there and go find a tavern to have a beer. Better yet, several beers.

After the drinks were poured and Cutter was in one of the overstuffed leather chairs, Amanda's father walked to the door, closed and locked it. "Winston," he started. Uh oh, when they use that name, it is never good. Her father continued, "I have to ask you a question and I apologize if it is uncomfortable for you."

"Go ahead." Cutter was beginning to get pissed all over again.

"Are you the father of the child Amanda bore?" Dead serious. You have got to be fucking kidding me. The child she "bore"? What kind of question is that?

Cutter was very pleased with his self-restraint. "No, sir. I didn't meet Amanda until after she was pregnant."

"Please keep your voice down, Winston." Appar-

147

ently Cutter wasn't exhibiting the self-restraint he thought he was. "But good. Good. That's what Amanda told us." Gee, she doesn't have your trust, even at her age? "Her mother and I would like to thank you for helping her through her difficult times. Perhaps, some gift might be in order."

It took every bit of Cutter's control, but he said, quietly and politely, "No, thank you, sir. That is totally unnecessary. This drink is quite enough." Cutter had never been more serious in his life. He got up and left the room. He asked Amanda if she wanted to go downtown and get a beer. She declined. He excused himself, told them he would be back in an hour, and drove to the nearest bar where he had back-to-back boilermakers. He didn't like boilermakers, but they were the quickest way to the place he wanted to go.

The rest of the weekend was not as bad. They spent some time with some of Amanda's high school chums. She was different, more relaxed. Like stepping back in time put things in perspective. The birthday party was subdued but pleasant. He got her a bracelet and she said she liked it. The one she told her sister to tell Cutter she wanted. Cutter was never one to pass up a suggestion. They drove back to the Quad Cities Sunday evening. She was quiet. He sensed her grow more withdrawn the closer they got to home.

"Cutter, can you drop me off at my place and not stay? I think I need to be alone for a while. I'll call you tomorrow."

She called four days later. "Thanks for being so

understanding. I'm better. Let's go downtown and get some pizza tomorrow, okay?"

"You bet," was all he could answer.

Then they went right back to their routine. The next time they spent anytime apart was four months later when she went to a teachers' conference in Des Moines. This time when she returned, the first thing she said was, "Cutter, we need to talk." Cutter, like everyone else in the whole fucking world, knew that was not a sentence you wanted to hear. He had expected it for a long time but now that it was here, he didn't dread it any less.

"Okay."

"I think we should see other people."

"Okay."

"Really? You think so too?" She was surprised by his reaction. Made it so much easier.

"It's time," was all he said.

"Buy me dinner," she told him,

"Okay." He took her to the Boat House. She was starved. Or famished. He couldn't remember which one came first. Dinner pleased him. There was no unmentioned weight on them. He took her home, got out of the car, kissed her on the check and said, "Goodbye."

A week later she called him, wanted to know if he wanted to have dinner. "Sure." A week after that, they were back to their routine. Two weeks after that, she told him, "Cutter, we need to talk."

"I thought we already did. I assumed you wanted

to go your own way, so I let you. You came back. What? Did you think you missed something? That it wasn't going to be that easy to get rid of me?"

She was sheepish. "I guess so."

"Go. Find what you need to find. Come back if you want. I won't promise I'll wait, but you never know." He kissed her on the cheek and said, "Good-bye." Again.

This time he didn't hear from her. According to friends, she started dating a principal from Cedar Rapids she'd met at the teachers' conference. At the end of the school year, she called him and told him she was moving to Cedar Rapids. He wished her luck. She said thanks and wished him luck as well.

In his head, he knew it was the only outcome. He tried to make his head convince his heart. Was mostly unsuccessful for a while. He went out on dates, rarely more than twice. Tried to bed a girl. She told him that it was okay, "It happens to everyone." Well, fuck, it never happened to me before. He was sad.

Quit his job at the ad agency because he thought a change of pace might help. Took a job working in a pro shop at a golf course. It was boring work, but he got to play a lot of golf. Collected hundreds of golf balls on early morning walks on the course. Slowly, he adjusted, managed to find his old happy self. Even when he heard Amanda was marrying the principal. All for the best. Worked his way into club management. Months passed. Two years' worth of months.

"Mr. Williams, this is Molly." A call on his cell phone.

"I'm sorry. Molly who?"

"Amanda's sister. Amanda Reagan."

"Oh, hi, Molly. I remember you. You thought I was cute. I remember every girl who says that. What's going on? How's Amanda?"

"I'm in town. Could we meet for a drink?"

"Are you old enough?" He tried to do the math in his head.

"No, but you are. Tell me when and where." He suggested a place and time. Met her there. She recognized him, he didn't recognize her. Went through the ordeal of ordering a beer.

"So tell me about Amanda. And you."

"Cutter, I hate to be the one to tell you, but Amanda died."

Cutter felt the earth lurch below him. Spilled his almost full beer. He couldn't help himself. The tears welled in his eyes and he choked back a sob. Molly got up and put her arms around his shoulders. She was not as surprised by his reaction as he was. He got up to walk out of the bar, telling her, "Stay here. I'll be back in a few minutes." He was gone for twenty minutes. She waited.

"Tell me what happened."

Molly asked, "When did you last hear from her?"

Cutter thought for a moment and answered, "She called to tell me she was moving to Cedar Rapids. That was the last time I actually spoke to her. Mutual friends who kept in touch with her told me she was getting married. That was a couple of years ago, I guess. I hadn't heard anything since then. Thought about her occasionally but never got around to asking anyone how she was. I guess I should have." He didn't want to admit that he thought of little else for a long, long time and thought it too unmanly to inquire about her among their friends.

"So how did she die? Accident? Did she get sick?"

"Maybe you need the gaps filled in first," Molly started. "The guy she married, Nick, was, is, a really terrific guy. We all loved him. He was good to and good for Amanda. He was a little older, like most of her boyfriends had been. Amanda wanted to have a baby right away. Nick wasn't wild about the idea since they had just gotten married and thought they needed some time for just the two of them, but Amanda was insistent."

Cutter interrupted, "And we all know how Amanda was when she was insistent." He smiled at the memory.

Molly continued her story. She told Cutter how they had tried to get pregnant for six months before they went to the doctor. Amanda had remained upbeat and appeared to be very happy, with Nick, with her marriage, with her life. She was teaching first graders in a public school and loved the job. No more fucking Fenton to deal with. Cutter chuckled when Molly said this, wondering how far that guy's reputation had actually spread.

The doctor said Nick was fine but they had to do an exploratory surgery on Amanda. Her "working parts", as Molly described them, had been damaged during the birth of the child she gave up for adoption.

"So you know about that?" Cutter asked her.

"Oh, yeah, she told me about the same time she told Nick, before they got married. I had already kind of figured it out on my own, though. Nick was okay with it. He really is a good guy."

"Sounds like it," Cutter said, a bit grudgingly.

Molly went on to explain there was nothing the doctors could do to repair the damage. Nick suggested they adopt a child. Amanda was completely against that idea. She screamed at Nick when he brought it up. Over the next six months or so, she became more despondent. Would go into times when she wouldn't talk to anyone.

She got it into her head that she could get her baby back from the adoptive parents. She came back to the Quad Cities, trying to find out what she could. The records were sealed of course. She hired a lawyer to get them unsealed. It didn't work. By then Amanda had become both sullen and angry. Threw Nick out of their house. Their families staged an intervention of sorts which only pissed her off more. But she was finally convinced to go see a doctor. Who did nothing except prescribe pills.

After a few months, the medication seemed to outside observers to have the intended impact. Amanda was pleasant and Nick was welcomed back. She wasn't happy, but certainly less maniacal. She quit talking about babies. They all thought she was going to be okay.

"She called in sick one day, said she had the flu. Nick called her at noon and she sounded sleepy, but said she was feeling better. When he got home, he found her in her bed. On the nightstand, the bottle with her meds was empty and a bottle of vodka half empty." At this point, Molly started crying and it was Cutter's turn to put his arms around her shoulders. They remained like that for several minutes before she continued.

"Thanks. Amanda always claimed you were a really great guy." It made Cutter smile.

Cutter asked, "Was it accidental?"

"No. There was a note. Hand written. It said she was sorry for screwing up everybody's lives, she apologized to Nick and to me, but not to our parents. It ended with the line 'There was only one person who could have fixed this and he didn't'. We assumed she meant the father of her child, though mom said it was our dad and blamed him. They had quite a fight over it."

Cutter thought there were several people she might be referring to. Certainly her dad or the father of the child, possibly Nick, though that sounded unlikely, more likely Terry. Most likely, she was talking about him, Cutter Williams, who could have asked her to marry him so she could have kept the baby. He pushed the thought from his head. It was too painful.

"You alright?" Molly asked.

"Well, no. But I will be. Thank you for letting me know. Is there anything I can do for you or the family?"

"Oh, no. We are all coping. It's been a few months now. I just thought you should know."

He told her thank you. He meant it.

The first time he felt it, Cutter was sitting at his desk three months later. He suddenly felt like he could not breathe. An elephant was sitting on his chest. He'd taken CPR; he knew this must be a heart attack. He chewed a couple of aspirin and realized there was no pain, just the pressure. Suddenly, he couldn't sit still. He paced back and forth and as long as he kept moving, the pain stopped. So he kept moving.

The third time it happened, he was driving the car and was afraid he was going to pass out and have a wreck, so he pulled to the curb and called an ambulance. Ended up in the emergency room where they ran a series of tests. The results were all negative so he was diagnosed with extreme stress and given a sedative. His brother picked him up at the hospital and took him to their parents' house. The following day he went to his own doctor who prescribed exercise, diet, relaxation techniques and pills, "just to get you over the tough spots."

He also strongly suggested that Cutter might want to figure out what was causing the stress. Job problems? Girl problems? Money problems? Cutter ignored everything but the pills for several months, learned to work around the panic attacks, hide how bad he was feeling from family and friends. Until he was driving back from a golf course in north central Iowa, fifty miles from nowhere and he suddenly could no longer drive. He got out of the car and paced for a while and got back behind the steering wheel. He shook so violently he had to get out and walk around some more. He just couldn't do it. Finally, he had to call his brother Jim to come get him.

He went to a shrink. Spent a couple of months in weekly sessions and learned a lot about himself. Most importantly, that while he had refused to think about it, he had blamed himself for Amanda's death and the attacks were a means of self-punishment. He got better.

He bought the Wrangler he always wanted and went on vacation. Took a part time job teaching English at a junior college. Gave himself a break. Started taking serious care of Cutter.

SIXTEEN

Sandy looked at Cutter, trying to make his story fit somehow, but it just wouldn't mesh. Hers and Clint's situation was entirely different. While Cutter finished his story, she rolled over in her mind everything she had been told by these men on this boat. How could anyone, Clint most of all, want to do harm to her child. My child. My child.

Whenever Sandy walked into a room, she assumed, until proven otherwise, she was the smartest person in the room. It rarely happened. These men were smart, plenty smart. But not as smart as she was. She knew it. They didn't. Which pretty much proved her point. Maybe she needed to start thinking with her head and not her vagina, if that was where the fairy tale ending was coming from.

Cutter stopped talking, but he seemed to be somewhere else. This was sure not the Cutter she knew. Sandy looked at him and waited for him to come out of his reverie. As she waited, she replayed Cutter's story about Amanda in her head and began to understand what he was trying to tell her. When he finally looked up at her, she smiled and asked, "So, what do you think I should do?"

"I don't know. You need to worry about yourself, I think. I'm seriously pissed about you guys fucking up *la cosa nostra*, but I'm with you on this."

She thought for a moment and said softly, "That's just what I was thinking, Cutter." And then much more firmly, "Exactly what I was thinking."

She dismissed Cutter. He asked her, "Should I say anything to Clint?"

"Not necessary." She hesitated. "No. Wait. Tell him to sneak down when he can and meet me in my cabin. Okay?"

"If that's what you want."

"It is."

Two minutes later he was back on the fishing deck where Clint was in the chair, playing a fish that was obviously not very large. Clint shot Cutter a look that said "Well?" Cutter held up a finger indicating Clint should finish his fishing, nothing urgent. It took Clint only two more minutes to reel in the small false albacore. He ceded the chair to Ken, since one of the trolling lines already had another hit and turned to Cutter.

"Well, what did she say? She on board?"

Cutter shook his head. "I'm not sure what she's thinking. She said you are to sneak down and meet her in her cabin as soon as you can."

"Great, Cutman. You're the best. Thanks." With that, Clint went first to find Lynn, who was coming up from their cabin, towel over her shoulder, book and

Bloody Mary in her hands. She looked at Clint and saw he had on his business face and her smile faded. "Oh, Clint, don't tell me you want another meeting. Do I have to go? We only have a few more hours out here and I want to get some sun."

"Oh, no, Babe. You go ahead. I just have to check with Sandy on a couple of things. No more meetings until we're back on land. Get some sun."

She transferred the book from her right hand to her armpit, reached down and gave his package a little squeeze and smiled. When he smiled in return, she added, "Maybe before we get back, we'll have time to check out that motion of the ocean thing," and winked at him. She went on up, he went on down.

A light tap on the door. "Yes?"

"Can I come in?" Clint asked, unusually meek.

"Yes."

Clint opened the door and walked in, straight over to Sandy, arms apart to embrace her. She put her hand on his chest, gently patting it and told him, in that wonderful soft voice she used sometimes, "Not now. I need to make sure I understand what you want and need. We'll be back on land soon enough and have this all behind us. We'll have plenty of time for other things."

"Well, what did Cutter tell you?" Clint asked.

"I need to hear it from you," she answered.

Clint began to feel like maybe he was standing on very slippery ice and needed to take each step carefully.

"Well, first, I love you. More than anything." She interrupted him, again in that soft voice, "I love you, too."

Thank god, this is going to be easier than I thought. "You know I want to marry you and have kids, but we can't screw up our future. I think you should have an abortion, but I know you don't want that. Maybe how we do this is you take a leave of absence to go, let's see, take some six month course at some university, and then when you return the election will be over and I can get a divorce and we'll get married then."

"Are you going to tell Lynn now?"

The slippery ice feeling again. "Oh. I don't think we can do that. No telling how she would react." He recalled the rusty razor blade threat.

"Okay." She patted him on the chest again, but this time let Clint hold her. She was shocked, more than she ever had been, how quickly an emotion could just evaporate and be replaced by another. It made her angry and sad, but she felt in control and that felt very, very good.

"Is it okay if I talk to Ken about this?" she asked.

"Uh, yeah. I guess so. He knows, but why do you want to talk to him?" Why did the ice keep returning?

"I need to make sure that in the event something would happen to me during all this, our child would be returned to you. I don't think I can trust any other lawyer with this. Do you?"

Clint relaxed, "Oh, yeah, good point. Excellent point. You should talk to him as soon as we get back to land."

"I still have time this morning and I want to get

this done. Would you tell him to come down and bring his legal pad with him, please? I don't feel like going up top quite yet. Besides, when we get back maybe you can send Lynn shopping or something, huh? This pregnancy seems to have affected my hormones and they are making me, what, even hornier than usual." She smiled.

This may work out just fine, Clint thought. In fact, this may be great. Just get to November and then everything will work out. And she won't have to go far away, someplace I can go visit her often. Take care of her hormonal needs. Keep Lynn quiet. Pat will like this. Cutter will come around. And Ken is always in my corner. Damn, Clinton Brandsgard, you are the man.

He hugged her one more time. When he stepped back, she patted him on the chest and he turned to go. As he went through the door, she reminded him to send Ken down.

When Clint got back topside, he discovered that the fishing rigs had been stowed and that the *Debbie Lee* was heading back to port. It was still a four or five hour trip but fishing was over. Clint felt so good, he almost beat his chest. Cutter wasn't around—he wanted to thank him again—but Lynn was on the front deck sunning, Pat was on his laptop at the shaded table outside and Ken was sitting on a deck chair, drinking a boat drink, wearing his return of the triumphant fisherman outfit, the orange Hawaiian shirt, white linen pants and his Hatteras cap. As always, a true fashionista.

Clint flashed a thumbs-up to Pat, who nodded in

return. Quietly he said to Ken, "Hey Kenny, could you help Sandy with a little legal thing she needs? Shouldn't take you long, but she really wants to do it now."

Ken did not smile. Curtly, "I suppose."

"She's in her cabin. I told her I would send you down. You're the man."

Ken got up, drink in hand, and padded down the steps and back to Sandy's cabin, knocked and entered when she said, "Come in."

"What can I do for you?" he asked her.

"Did you really tell Clint last night that he should work this out with me, aside from the politics?"

"Yes. This should be between the two of you."

"But what do you think, really?" she wanted to know.

"That you guys were incredibly stupid and should accept responsibility for what has happened." Ken Riley, master of tact. Add it to his list. "Fair enough," she replied. She told him what she wanted. What he was to write and put into legal form. As she spoke, he went from shaking his head to nodding his head to grinning. She ended with, "I have two questions for you. One, is the governor's office worth that much to Huntsman, and, two, if it is, can you call him from here?"

"Oh, it's worth a lot more than that to him. I can call him. Will call him. I'm sure the captain has a sat phone I can use. Huntsman will not be happy. But I think he'll agree. He's too deep in to find another horse to ride. He knows he won't get a chance like this again."

"Good. Do it." Not quite as an order. But the effect was the same.

When Ken returned to the deck, Clint raised his eyebrows as a question. Ken answered with a thumbs-up. Clint and Pat both nodded. Ken went up to the pilot's house where he asked Captain Jefferson if he could use the sat phone, explaining, in very general terms, the urgency of the request. No problem. Ken made the call from there. They had to find Mr. Huntsman, but he was on the line in less than two minutes.

Ken told him what he needed. Huntsman ranted for a good three minutes. Then agreed. Ken reminded him that Paul could not be involved. Again, Huntsman was pissed, but agreed. Huntsman told him it would take an hour or so, but would email him when it was done. Told Ken he wanted a copy of the agreement by return email. Ken agreed.

Ken went back to his cabin to get his laptop, found Cutter there. Cutter said, "Well?"

Ken answered with, "Cutter, how 'bout you and me, we go get drunk tonight?" Enigmatic. Ken Riley, man of a thousand faces. Cutter did not know what to make of the response but before he could ask, Ken said, "Go get me a Bloody Mary, okay?" Cutter did, found Ken hunched over his laptop, left the drink and went up on deck.

An hour later, Ken reported back to Sandy and showed her the document. She asked for a couple of changes, he made them right there and then went aft to use the boat's printer, where he made three copies.

Took all three to her. She signed all three and asked Ken to have Clint come down. He did.

"Clint, sit down." Uh oh, this was not her soft voice.

"Sandy, honey," he started.

"Shut up. Listen. I'm only going to go through this once. This is the deal. You take it or leave it."

He interrupted, "Deal? What do you mean deal? What if I don't like the 'deal'?"

"Then I march upstairs and have a chat with Lynn and we'll see if she wants to deal."

The ice had reappeared and he had fallen flat on his ass.

"I am going to resign my job. You may keep and use my idea on the kids' health issue. And anything else I have worked on. I am going to go away. I am going to have our baby and raise it. By myself. I will be silent about the identity of the father. You will have no responsibility for the child. Likewise, you will have no rights as a parent. You will have no contact with my child. In return, I will be paid the equivalent of the costs to raise a child, up to and including college."

All he could think to say was, "I don't have that kind of money. You know that."

"Shut up. That's been taken care of. Your sponsor, though now I should say your owner, the right honorable Gerald Huntsman, has already transferred the money and will release it after we sign this agreement. You go to the statehouse. I go wherever I choose. Understood? Agreed?"

Clint ran through it in his head. Wanted to ask Pat. Not Ken. He had fucked him over, joining forces with this bitch. Pat was right. Better to be done with her.

"Fine." He signed the copies of the agreement without even reading it. "You bitch," was all he could muster.

"Spoken like the true gentleman you are. Get out."

After he left her, Sandy packed her things in her backpack and went to find Ken. He completed the transaction with Huntsman and told her the funds were transferred. Ken hugged her. He went to find Cutter to explain to him what had happened. Cutter nodded and smiled and said to Ken, "Hey, why don't we get drunk tonight. See if Jordair and Samantha want to join us. Hell, Kenneth, I'll even let you buy."

An hour out of port, everyone was on deck. Lynn came down from the sunning deck and announced, "I am so bored. When do we get back?" She was ignored.

Half an hour later, Jordair asked them all to get their bags packed so he could move them to the deck for unloading. Also asked them to double check the whole boat to make sure they weren't leaving anything behind. They did as instructed, no conversations going on at all. Unusually quiet group, Jordair thought.

Jordair and Samantha got the *Debbie Lee* tied up and secured and lowered the gangplank. Jordair put all the bags on the dock and Captain Jefferson thanked them all for the great trip and wished them well. Reminded them it was customary to tip the mates. Finished with, "Cutter, you may want to stick around to see if that fish of yours is a record maker. Up to you."

"You bet. I'll throw my stuff in my car and be right back." Cutter followed Lynn off the boat. She walked directly toward the ships store. He went to his Jeep.

The others walked up the gangplank and onto the dock. Clint was the last one off, after giving tips to Jordair and Samantha. Sandy met him as he stepped onto the dock where she put her hand lightly on his chest. She smiled at him and said, in her soft voice again, "I quit." And shoved him into the water.

Twenty minutes later they had unloaded the barracuda and hauled it to the scales. It weighed in at ninety-one pounds and a few ounces, which was, after they checked, large enough to be a record. Cutter and the crew and captain all posed for pictures with it. Cutter was struck by an idea.

"Captain Jefferson, I have a proposition for you."

"What?"

"If I can turn this catch of ours into additional business by using the media, what share of the increased profits would you give me?"

"Uh, twenty per cent," Jefferson offered.

"Make it twenty-one and it's a deal," Cutter countered.

"Okay. But why twenty-one?"

"Seven per cent for each of the three mates. I want to be the third mate."

"We can talk, son. We can talk." Jefferson offered his hand to Cutter and they shook.

Cutter got back to his Jeep and found Sandy sitting in it.

"Hey, sailor. Give a girl a ride?"

EPILOGUE

Nearly four years later, Cutter was sitting in the yard at his parents' house. All the kids were getting ready for the annual Williams Easter egg hunt, creating the general chaos which always earmarked the event. Watching reminded him of the Easter Amanda had joined him there and how happy she had acted on that afternoon. He thought back over the years since. A long time, but sometimes it all seemed to have flown by. Thought about how he had ended up at city hall, and then, in no small part because of Amanda, as a mate on the *Debbie Lee*.

Three days after Clintfest on the boat, he met with Tom Jefferson. The captain had had a couple of charters scheduled over the next two days, which was fine with Cutter since it gave him time to do a little research and work. He mocked together a website, wrote an article for Tom's byline for submission to fishing magazines about landing a record fish, complete with photos, and did some work on a potential ad campaign for the *Debbie Lee*.

Captain Jefferson didn't know much about any of

those things, but when he realized he would get those things for free just by hiring a replacement mate, he thought they were great. He had to hire a mate anyway. Besides, Jordair liked Cutter a lot and Samantha thought he was okay. Done deal. Cutter got a small salary, free place to sleep on board, food when they were on the water, and tips. To the captain's surprise, business did pick up, enough for him to raise his charter rates. Seems every Midwestern big game fisherman wanted to sail on a charter that landed record fish.

By the end of the season in November, Cutter's twenty-one percent was enough that it amounted to forty per cent of a mate's salary for each of the three of them. Jordair and Samantha went from liking Cutter to thinking he was the best guy ever. Not to mention, he had drawn the crappy jobs. Like cleaning out the bilge, scrubbing down decks and filling ice chests. He went home to visit, got caught up on the news from city hall. The mayor had easily won reelection and had announced a new initiative about children's health care. The paper and the television stations made it sound like those two things all but insured Clinton Brandsgard would be the next governor of the State of Iowa.

Cutter spent the winter months working as a starter at a private golf course in Florida and doing some sales work for the *Debbie Lee*. Heard from Sandy that she had had her baby, a little girl whom she had named Jordan. Her divorce had gone through at the end of summer and since she asked for only half of what they owned and no alimony, it was uncontested. Ken had handled it for her. Paul didn't even show up at court. She and Jordan were living in Des Moines where she was working part time for the State Department of Education.

Cutter returned to the Outer Banks for the season, this time as an experienced hand. It was hard work but he liked it. Jordair and Samantha were both back, though in June one of the guys who chartered the boat swept Samantha off her feet and she left with him. He was rich. And liked the taste of bluefish. It worked out, leastwise the last Cutter had heard. He wrote a couple of fishing articles and stories he sold to magazines and started fancying himself as a new age Hemingway. But by the end of his second season, he was getting bored and tired of the limitations of island life.

After Thanksgiving, he told Captain Jefferson he would not return the next year and wished him luck. Said goodbye to Jordair. Told him to look him up in the Midwest. Jordair only laughed. He sold the Jeep and packed up his few belongings and sent them to his parents' house. Got a bus ticket to Iowa. Geez, thirty-four years old, I have nothing to show for it and I'm moving back in with my parents. His parents didn't exactly greet the news with enthusiasm, though they were happy to have him through the holidays. A guest in his own house. Well, not his house, but he had grown up there. After three days, guests were like fish, they both began to stink. Something Cutter understood better than most.

Two days after Christmas, Cutter got a call, "Cutter, Happy Holidays!"

"Hey, Sandy, the same to you. How the hell are you? How's that baby?" Cutter was excited to hear her voice.

"We're great. In town visiting. Heard you were here as well. Want to join Jordan and me for lunch?"

They met the next day. She had a beer waiting for him. "Aw. You remembered," was his greeting. They hugged, caught up on each other's lives and Cutter played with Jordan.

"Cutter, I've been offered a contract with a statewide think tank to do some policy wonk stuff for them. They do work for governments and for candidates. I wondered if you might want to join me."

He looked at her and shook his head. "I don't know. The last time you bought me a beer and offered me a job, look how it turned out." But he was smiling. And again, she had come along just when he needed to pay the rent. "Sure. Just no more assholes, okay?"

"Deal!" They shook on it.

Clint had announced his campaign for governor, an announcement that had been so expected it generated little interest. Other than by a few thoughtful media commentators and columnists who were starting to voice concern over the viability of Clint's children's health program. He had managed to get the state legislature to make the changes in the law he needed for it, but the program was now on its third director and sputtering badly. No one could see any benefits. Lots of committees, lots of meetings, lots of press releases but no tangible results. At the point he announced his candidacy, only a few in the press were asking questions. When Clint and his campaign manager, Pat Kovachik, decided to make taking that program, the one that didn't exist, statewide, the media heavens opened up and rained on the campaign's parade.

Sandy and Cutter watched with barely controlled, but professional, glee from their offices in Des Moines. Clint's campaign was a train wreck. It got worse. Clint's wife had gotten drunk at a formal affair in Des Moines and had said to a young black man in a tuxedo, "Boy, go get me another drink." The young man was the chief clerk for the Chief Justice of the State Supreme Court. He got her the drink. It was all recorded and on the internet before morning.

By the end of summer, the campaign funds completely dried up and Kovachik threw in the towel, withdrawing his candidate from the race. It marked the end of both of their political careers.

As the kids gathered on the starting line for the egg hunt, Cutter experienced one of those uncontrollable associative tricks the mind occasionally plays. His thoughts of Amanda led him to ponder what it would have been like if Amanda and her daughter were here and what their lives would be like. Which led him to wonder about the girl's life today. It would no doubt have saddened him to know the girl lived not ten minutes away from his parents' house and while her parents were wealthy and provided her with everything a kid could ever want, she was mostly ignored and lonely.

The Williams family children started the mad rush for the candy and eggs and Grandma Williams' prize eggs, which were worth cold, hard cash. Cutter came out of his reverie, reached over and patted Sandy on the knee and said, "I better go help Jordan or the big kids will run right over her." He knew this wasn't true, but all these years he had wanted to join in the hunt like his brothers and sisters did with their kids.

"Okay, have fun," Sandy said, though Cutter was already into the fray, tugging Jordan towards the best hiding places.

She turned to Cutter's brother Jim and said, "You know, Cutter has asked me to marry him."

"We know." Jim answered. "In fact we think it's wonderful."

After they had worked together for a year or so, Cutter had finally asked Sandy on an official date. She had laughed at him, until she realized he was serious. She went. It worked out. It was not the blind passion either had had earlier, but it was terrific. They marveled at the fact they had never figured it out before.

Sandy continued, "Well, before I say yes, I need to know a couple of things."

"Sure," Jim said, grinning from ear to ear. "What?"

"Did Cutter have a pet chicken when he was a kid?"

"Not that I knew about. We had a couple of cats and a dog. That was it. Mom hates birds."

She laughed and went on, "So how did he get his nickname?"

"Funny you should ask today," Jim answered.

"Why is that funny?"

"When Cutter was about three, the family got all dressed up and went to mass on Easter morning. The Williams family was lined up in their pew, the pride of Mom and Dad. When it was time for the priest's sermon, he came to the pulpit, looked down on the congregation and spread his arms wide, a theatrical gesture to let everyone know he was about to begin the most important sermon of the year. Instead, in the seconds before he could speak, in the dead quiet of anticipation, there is this loud, very loud, fart. Everyone in church laughed. Except my mother, who realized it had come from her brood. Anything the priest had to say was lost. The only thing folks remembered was the flatulence. The Easter Fart became congregation history. Mom was pissed. At the end of mass, she pulled us outside and demanded to know who had done it. We all told her it was Win. Told her, Win was the cutter. She yelled at him. He was kind of lost, he had no idea that he had done it. If he had done it. But Cutter became his nickname. He doesn't remember how he got the name. We won't tell him."

Sandy finally quit laughing and asked, "So was Cutter the kid who did it?"

Jim smiled and told her, "Nah. It was me."

174

ACKNOWLEDGMENTS

Generally speaking, writing is a solitary endeavor. But getting started, staying focused and finishing require a lot of help. And it works out even more help is needed to turn a story into a book. I want to thank those who made it both possible and fun. Deborah Varner, my wife, who fervently encouraged me to sit down and actually write and acted as my muse and day to day (and final) editor. She was especially helpful making me see what was not good and what needed to be changed. Any mistakes are mine, and mine alone. She did a yeoman's job and I can't thank her enough. Jordan Callaham, Jake Barney and Samantha Varner all gave of their time, reading and making helpful suggestions. Additionally Samantha provided invaluable help with commentary. Again, any mistakes are mine, not hers. Vicki Moon Spiegel did the artwork and the layout for the cover. She is nothing short of brilliant. Google is probably the best research assistant a guy can have. When you're sitting in a tiny apartment in Paris writing, only Google can tell you about fishing boats and record fish and little known restaurants. I trust Google was accurate. I also want to thank Tad Barney for his assistance. Finally, Samantha became the *de facto* publisher, doing immense amounts of research and work to turn the story into a book. Thanks to you all—you make me want to do it again.

Made in the USA
Lexington, KY
23 June 2015